A Family Christmas Story

by Lillian Francken

ISBN-10: 1478244119
ISBN-13: 978-1478244110

Dedicated to my family,
Who inspires me!

Other Books by Lillian Francken:

The Twelfth of Never
Tetris
Omega Factor
Rustic Roads
Till Death Do Us Part
Blue Moon Rising
Wednesday's Child
A Family Christmas Story
We Come In Peace
The Curiosity Shop
All About Love

Other Books under pen name J.J. Franck
Raven
Into the Darkness
Someone to Watch Over Me
Shadows into the Night
1501 Parcher Place

Visit my website for more information about Lillian Francken

http://lillianfrancken.weebly.com/

Chapter 1

Noon rush hour in the Loop was always a hassle. Usually, Megan Montgomery ate at her desk, but she wanted to have lunch with Tillie, a friend she met in college. The two moved to Chicago five years earlier right out of college. It was the only opportunity she had to give Tillie her Christmas gift, as she would be going home in a few days to spend the holiday with her family. Megan hurried past window shoppers and wondered why people waited until the last minute to do their Christmas shopping. Megan had it on her Franklin Planner to start in October. She lived by her planner, and it was her way of keeping organized.

It had been a busy morning at work. The rumors of another layoff looming before the New Year hampered a happy end to the fiscal year in a few weeks. Bank of America had seen troubled times in recent years. She made a point of not reading the articles in the Wall Street Journal, as they always depressed her. The one favorable state of affairs going for her was that her department was the only one that's budget was in the black. So she felt confident that she would still have a job when she got back from her vacation and even into the coming new year.

Megan hurried along West Adam Street to the Rhapsody Restaurant. She had chosen that restaurant for lunch because that was where Robert made reservations for their New Year's Eve celebration and she never liked going anyplace without scouting it out first. Some people called her a control freak, but Megan never wanted to leave anything to chance. She wanted to be prepared. Megan had already done a virtual tour of it online. Judging by the pictures, she was intrigued and wanted to see for herself how elegant it was. She was surprised at the prices on the menu. Megan knew that Robert had to have something on his mind to spend that kind of money on an evening out.

Megan was so deep in thought about the Rhapsody that she did not notice Tillie across the street until she heard her name being called.

"Megan!"

Megan glanced up in time to see Tillie waving her arms wildly to get her attention. Megan quickly crossed the street and hoped no police officer was in view. They frowned on jaywalking, especially during the busy noonday traffic. But she'd never had the misfortune to find out what the fine would be for such a misdeed.

"I'm glad you could get out early," Megan said.

"Hey, it wasn't easy. You know how crazy people get this time of year. But even in Scrooge's time, you had time off for lunch."

"Tell me about it. I hated to ask off the extra days over the holiday period, even though I have the time coming."

Tillie rolled her eyes as she frowned. "I don't know why they need to get their pound of flesh out of you before the end of the year."

"I know, my boss has been a real Ebenezer Scrooge lately. I've been waiting for the three ghosts to show up to teach him the meaning of Christmas," Megan smirked as she rolled her eyes.

They both laughed, knowing full well it was just a story. One could only hope there was some truth to how people regained their holiday spirit. Megan looked at the Christmas displays in the windows. The active ones were the most interesting, as they watched a train full of toys slowly move from one display window to the next. She remembered past Christmases where her father would drive downtown, and they would walk along Third Street and view all the displays after dark. It was a magical time for her and a time in her life she cherished, that and took rides to see how everyone decorated their houses. Amazing how one neighbor always outdid the next, making the electric company a bundle of money during the holiday season. It occurred to her that it was probably someone who worked for the electric company who started that tradition. She put that thought out of her head because she was starting to become cynical.

They quickly walked to the next display window when Tillie turned to Megan. "Did you get your Christmas bonus yet?"

Megan coughed, almost choking at the thought. "Christmas bonus? After this year's disaster, no one was expecting a bonus? I'm lucky I still have a job to come back to in January."

The two young women stopped in front of the jeweler's window next to the Rhapsody Restaurant. Megan glanced at her reflection for a moment. Her shoulder-length hair blew in the breeze. Her hazel eyes looked longingly at all the sparkling diamonds on the other side of the glass. They were all laid out on red and green velvet, setting off their beauty even more. The sudden burst of sunlight reflecting off the window caused Megan to wince as she shielded her eyes from the glare. Once Megan regained her composure she stared at the array of engagement and wedding rings. She was lost in a daydream, wondering if her day would ever come, and then she sighed.

Tillie laughed at Megan with a mocking grin on her face. She knew what Megan was thinking, and she liked teasing her.

Megan turned to Tillie. "What's your problem anyway?" she said.

"You know he's going to ask you, so why are you worried?" Tillie laughed. "He's only had eyes for you ever since you guys met."

"How can you be so sure? We've been dating only a year. He's never really talked about me meeting his family or mentioned a future together."

"Trust me, I know."

Megan glanced at the time. "Hey, we better get going. I promised my boss I wouldn't be late again."

Tillie was glad to stop looking at the rings and feared Megan could see she knew more than she was letting on about Robert's intentions. If truth be known, it was she that Robert took to help pick out the engagement ring he was going to present to Megan on their New Year's Eve celebration.

They quickly hurried into the restaurant. Tillie suspected Megan knew something was up because why else pick the Rhapsody for lunch and then just happen to look at the window display at the jewelry store that Robert had purchased her ring from. It was just too coincidental. But she would play along with the charade. Besides, it was a free lunch because it was Megan's turn to buy.

The restaurant was filling up fast with noon-hour workers and shoppers, and they were ushered to the rear of the restaurant near a window. Megan was glad now that she called ahead and made reservations. It was pleasant enough, and Megan wondered why it was Robert's choice for their New Year's Eve celebration.

Megan ate her salad while Tillie picked the shredded cheese out of the salad with her knife and fork.

"I told them to hold the cheese. They always do that," Tillie snapped."

"You gave me the impression you never ate here before."

Tillie had a guilty look on her face. She did not want to tell her that she and Robert came here for a dry run before he made the reservations for New Year's Eve. Robert wanted everything to be perfect when he asked Megan to marry him, and Tillie was just trying to help out.

Tillie stuttered a moment and then caught herself. "I meant in general. Whenever I ask for something out of the ordinary, they never seem to listen."

"Then tell them to take it back," Megan snapped and then frowned. "I thought you liked cheese?"

"Not on my salad. I like things a certain way. Besides, I've heard when you send things back they spit in your food? No way would I ever send anything back," she mocked. "I'll just pick it out myself and not give the waitress a tip in the end."

"Oh, just shut up and eat it. Cheese is good for you."

"Easy for you to say, everything always goes your way."

Megan laughed. "I wish."

Tillie was desperate to change the subject. "Where's Robert going for Christmas?"

"I don't know. His parents are going to Europe for the holidays, and I get the impression he's avoiding the subject."

"Must be nice."

"That he doesn't know where he's spending Christmas or that his parents are spending the holiday in Europe?"

"You know what I mean."

"Hey, they worked hard for what they have," Megan said.

"What is it, ketchup or mustard that they were into?"

"It's ketchup, but I think they have their line of mustard under development now."

"You wouldn't know it to look at him. He sounds like any other poor schmuck I've met in the big city. If I had known he came from money, I'd have made a move on him myself." Tillie knew full well Robert was not her type. She just wanted to ruffle Megan's feathers.

Tillie glanced up at Megan. It was as if she just had an idea, but actually, it was something that Robert suggested she mentioned to Megan when they talked that morning.

"Why don't you invite him home with you?"

Megan looked at Tillie with wide eyes. "To my dysfunctional family? You have got to be kidding," she laughed.

She regarded Tillie with intense skepticism. Granted Tillie had never met her family personally, but Megan had shared horror stories about them in the past. It surprised her that Tillie would even suggest such an option. But the fact remained, and she knew it. There would eventually have to be a time when Robert would have to meet her family. She just was not ready for it yet.

"Everyone comes from some dysfunctional family. Don't sell yours short."

Megan shook her head. "You haven't met mine. Trust me, when you look up dysfunction in the dictionary, the word 'Dombrowski' is in parenthesis."

"Your last name is Montgomery," Tillie smirked.

"It's not my father's family that's the cause of all the problems."

Tillie studied Megan for the longest time. "So are you ever going to let him meet them?"

Megan fidgeted with her fork for a moment. She thought long and hard. It had been something that had bothered her for weeks.

"I thought that I'd invite him home for Easter," she sighed as she rolled her eyes. "The problem with Christmas is that it's my parents turn to host the Christmas open house. It would be overwhelming for him, to say the least. At Easter, there would just be my parents."

"Maybe he'll want to spend Easter with his family."

"I'll worry about that when the time comes, all I know is I don't want him with my family at Christmastime this year."

Tillie realized it was futile to pursue this further and Robert was on his own when it came to meeting Megan's parents. She only wished to be a fly on the wall when he tricked her into this first meeting. She knew Robert was not going to give up on this that quickly. Plus, the fact that he wanted to ask Megan's father for her hand in marriage. It sounded romantic, but given Megan's apprehension at Robert meeting her family, Tillie was not so sure this was a good idea just yet.

"Why isn't he in the family business?" Tillie asked, trying to change the subject.

"It isn't the family business as much as living in New York, I think."

"No one is ever happy with what they have. So when is he going to pop the question?" Tillie asked, knowing full well that Robert planned on doing so on New Year's Eve. She just wanted to know if Megan was onto his plans.

"I don't want even to go there," she said as she glanced at her watch. "I have to get going, or I'll be late getting back to work."

Megan was glad for the excuse to leave. Robert asking her to marry him was weighing heavily on Megan recently. She feared that maybe he was tired of her, given recent developments where she had the opportunity to meet his parents, but he chose not to introduce her to them. She quickly reached into her purse and tossed a bill on the table.

"Take care of it, will you?" she said to Tillie as she got up quickly and left.

Tillie glanced up, "No problem, and have a Merry Christmas if I don't talk to you before you leave."

"You too," Megan smiled, and then rushed off.

CHAPTER 2

Across town at the Bank of America office building on South Walker, Robert Murphy, vice president of operations, sat in his office inputting data into his laptop. It had been a busy morning for the young professional. Crunching the numbers for the year-end report that was due before the end of the year. Robert had been at the bank for more than eight years now. The bags under his eyes contested to the troubled times that had overtaken the industry of late. He was fortunate that his branch was in the black in recent years. It was all due to their careful screening of potential customers and keeping a tight reign on the lending practices they undertook.

Fred O'Connor, Robert's longtime friend, and co-worker, knocked on the door and just walked in and plopped himself down on the couch on the other side of the room. He lay for the longest time with his arms behind his head and shut his eyes.

"That bad?" Robert asked, leaning back in his chair and stretched his shoulders.

"A day from hell," Fred joked, opening his eyes and looked up at Robert.

"It always is just before Christmas."

"People squeezing their last bit of profit into the year. It was like squeezing blood from a turnip."

"That's why they call you a personal financial planner," Robert said sarcastically.

"Yeah, but why wait until the end of the year to want to sit down and try to put the year-end in the black when they should have been practicing fiscal management of their funds months ago."

"Think of it this way. You're keeping the economy going. And remember the commission that comes with it."

"Sometimes I think it's just not worth the effort. The hassle dealing with these people is driving me crazy. That's why I got off the Midwest Stock Exchange. Yeah, the money was good but jumping through hoops was never my cup of tea."

"Sounds like someone is feeling sorry for themselves today," Robert mocked.

Fred glanced at Robert. "You're a trust-fund baby, why don't you just sit back and enjoy it?"

Robert laughed. "There's more to life than sitting on your duff all day," he said, saving his spreadsheet and then closing his laptop.

"So you feel the need to get down and dirty in the trenches with us grunts?"

"It may surprise you, but I get more enjoyment putting in a hard day's work than doing nothing all day," Robert said.

Robert thought about all his boyhood friends who came from wealthy parents. They spent their summers at the country club. Whereas Robert, once his parents left the house for the day, spent his time with the yardman following him around and doing odd jobs for him.

Fred looked at his watch. He had been ready for lunch for hours now. But he had clients to deal with, and once he sent the last one on his way, he was not sticking around for one of those walk-in customers who only wanted to talk hypothetically for an hour or two. Then do nothing with the information he got for free.

"You ready for lunch? You did say you were treating for Christmas?" Fred quickly added.

"When is it ever going to be your turn to treat?"

Fred slowly got up and laughed. "I've got a wife and two mouths to feed."

"And all the excuses in the world to go with it."

In all actuality it was Robert's turn to treat, he just liked giving Fred the business about being a moocher. It was a game they'd played since their first meeting. Robert got up and grabbed the jacket off the coat rack while shaking his head as he followed Fred. Before leaving, he turned off the light and locked the door.

* * *

At the restaurant, Fred undressed the waitress with his eyes as she walked by. Robert snapped his fingers in Fred's face to get his attention.

"You're married, remember those two kids you were telling me about earlier?" Robert mocked.

"That doesn't mean I'm dead."

"It won't be like that for me," Robert snapped.

Fred turned and looked at Robert for a moment and then shook his head and laughed. "When are you going to ask Megan to marry you?"

"I had planned to pop the question New Year's Eve. But I still haven't met her parents. And I think it's important that I ask her father for her hand in marriage first."

"How romantic," Fred muttered with a sarcastic grin. And then stared at the waitress for a moment, but after a moment Fred quickly turned back to Robert. "What about her meeting your parents?"

Robert laughed. "And have her change her mind about marrying me after meeting them?"

"It can't be that bad."

"Hey, trust me, I'd run if I met them as prospective in-laws."

They were quickly seated and placed their orders. It didn't take long, and the food was brought out to them.

"So what are your plans?" Fred asked as the waitress set the plate of food in front of him.

Robert reached into his jacket pocket and pulled out the airline ticket. He handed it to Fred who quickly read the destination and then frowned.

"You're going to travel up in the boonies?"

"It isn't that far, only central Wisconsin."

"Isn't that Packer country?" Fred asked as if it was a warning about something dangerous.

"Remember, I'm not from around here like you. And Megan and I do not talk sports."

"I don't know, that was a criterion for me. She had to be a Bears fan."

Robert shook his head. He wondered how Fred could ever have become serious about anyone. But then Robert met his wife and the two played off each other all the time. Fred talked big, but in all actuality, Robert was sure he would have married Molly no matter who she rooted for on Sunday afternoon.

"All I know is I want to spend the rest of my life with Megan."

"You sure have it bad. I guess there's no talking you out of it," Fred added.

"I've got it covered. I'm going to surprise Megan."

"You like living dangerously?"

"She might be a little upset at first, but I'm sure she won't have a problem with it."

"You're going to have to e-mail me the outcome."

"I'm not taking the laptop," Robert said, which surprised Fred.

"It's going to be a vacation."

"I'm asking the woman I love to marry me. I don't need to take a laptop along for entertainment. Besides, I'll still have my smart phone, so I guess I could text you the outcome," Robert laughed.

"Can I see the ring?"

Robert reached into his pocket and handed Fred the black velvet box. Fred opened the box and then whistled. The Asscher diamond ring sparkled in the restaurant lights.

"Must have cost you a few bucks?"

Fred snapped the box shut and handed it back to Robert.

"You did insure it, didn't you?"

Robert rolled his eyes because Fred always seemed to think about money. He had not thought about the cost. All he wanted was Megan to be happy with the ring, and the four-karat cut seemed perfect for the setting. This was the first time he had ever proposed, and he wanted to do it right.

The two quickly ate their lunch, as there was still a lot of work left to do before the holiday break. Once the waitress gathered up their empty plates and topped off the coffee, Fred looked up at her.

"You can bring my friend the bill," he said and then glanced at his watch.

Robert just shook his head. "Did you ask Molly's father for her hand in marriage?" Robert asked, curious if he was doing the right thing, not knowing what to do, or who to ask really. Robert spent a lot of time on the Internet looking for the correct way to do this monumental task.

Fred just laughed. "Hell no!" he said. "You aren't going to be a dork and ask the old man for her hand, are you?"

Robert just shrugged his shoulders. "Why not?"

"Oh, man," Fred mocked. "You can always change your mind once you get there."

"Is that your only advice?" Robert asked.

"Trust me. It's not an easy task. Plus, there's the sad fact they don't know you. Has Megan even told them about you?"

"I'm not sure," Robert said with a concerned look on his face. In reality, every time he brought up the subject of her parents she would find a way to change the subject.

It had bothered him that she had a family wedding last month and the invitation was not extended to a friend. At least that was what Megan said. So he was not sure her family knew she was seeing anyone. He wondered now if she informed them that she was in a relationship. He felt they had been serious for some time. And as if a light bulb went off, it occurred to him at that moment. He had not broken the news to his parents that he had been seeing someone. And now the fact he planned to ask her to marry him over this holiday. He now wondered if they would have planned this European vacation or tried to get him home for the holiday so he could bring the girl that would be a part of their family home to meet them.

"Well, as I said, you can always change your mind."

"I have my mind made up to do this and do it right. Besides, I want to get off on the right foot with her family."

Fred shook his head while picking up the cup of coffee in salute to Robert, and then he gulped the hot liquid down.

"My only advice for you is run."

"Thanks a lot for your encouragement."

"So when you going to tell Megan you're coming with her?" Fred asked while he laughed at the absurdity of Robert's plan.

"I thought I'd just show up at the airport. I have a seat next to her on the plane."

"You have a death wish."

"I wouldn't say that."

"How do you think her parents are going to receive you?"

"I've got hotel reservations already. It isn't as if I'm expecting them to put me up, too."

The waitress interrupted their conversation and handed Robert the bill. He quickly reached into his wallet and gave her his credit card.

"Next time it is on you, for sure."

Fred turned to Robert and reluctantly offered his hand. "Congratulations. You know she's still going to have to meet your parents sooner or later."

"Later suits me just fine, and I'll cross that bridge when I get to it."

Once the waitress was back with the receipt, Robert signed it quickly, and the two got up and left.

CHAPTER 3

Christmas music played in the distance while colorful Christmas lights twinkled in the snow that fell. The Loop had always been a favorite place for Megan since coming to the city. The hustle and bustle of a busy city were so unlike the community in which she grew up, where neighbors still left their doors unlocked during the day, and everyone knew your name. She missed it sometimes, but not enough to give up her life in the city.

Robert and Megan had walked hand and hand for over an hour, stopping at Daley Plaza to stare up at Picasso's sculpture before going down State Street to view the window displays. As they passed a jewelry store, Robert purposely pulled Megan along, not wanting to stop and look at the beautiful rings in the display. Megan, sensing his hesitance at looking at engagement rings, appeared disappointed by his action and took it as a sign he apparently did not want to marry her just yet.

The reservations for the restaurant that Robert made were not far from Daley Plaza. Once it was in sight, he breathed a sigh of relief. Robert had been nervous when passing the different jewelry store displays. He feared he would spill the beans and ask for her hand before he made the pilgrimage to her family tomorrow. It was getting harder for him to keep his secret from Megan. He smiled when he saw the disappointment on her face. He only had one chance at doing this deed right, so he bit his tongue and kept his mouth shut.

Robert opened the door for Megan and ushered her inside where the hostess guided them to their table. When he made the reservations earlier that week, he asked for something off the beaten path. Robert was pleased when he saw the table in back with candles lit and the lights turned low. Soft Christmas music played in the background, putting the patrons in the holiday spirit. No sooner than they were seated, the waitress brought a bottle of Champagne that Robert had requested when making the reservations. He wanted everything to be perfect for what Megan thought was their last evening together before the holiday.

Now that Megan was in the right mood Robert took out a box from his jacket pocket, but it was not the box with a ring. It was a diamond pendant he bought because he knew she would be expecting something from him in the way of a Christmas gift. Again there was the look of disappointment on her face that he secretly enjoyed seeing because he now was sure she was expecting something else.

"I wanted to give you this before you leave tomorrow," he said, trying to hide his true feelings.

"I thought we agreed to celebrate Christmas when I got back," Megan replied, now a little angry with him because his gift was still at the apartment, unwrapped.

"Well, I just wanted you to have it before you leave for your parents."

Megan opened the box. There was both pleasure and disappointment on her face as it was not the ring she had hoped for, but instead, a beautiful diamond pendant that any woman would have died to have. She was angry with herself for wanting more. Knowing full well in time she was sure Robert would pop the question she so longed to hear. But for now, she would have to settle for the gift he gave her.

Robert took Megan's hand and kissed it longingly. As Megan took the pendant out of the box, Robert got up quickly and took it from her and proceeded to put it around her neck. Before sitting back down, he took the bottle of Champagne and poured two glasses and then quickly handed Megan one of the glasses. Once he sat back down, he lifted his glass and reached over and tapped it to Megan's.

"I want to celebrate our eleven-month anniversary."

"You should have waited to celebrate our year together."

"I have plans for that," Robert said, smiling sheepishly.

Megan had a gleam in her eye, knowing there might be hope after all. "You going to give me a hint?" Megan asked shyly.

"No. You'll have to wait."

"I wish we could have had Christmas together."

"You could always stay in town with me."

Megan rolled her eyes but then shook her head. She knew all too well that her parents would be disappointed if she did not come home for Christmas. It was a time of the year that her family always made a point of getting together. That was why she had mixed emotions about this year. She would have loved to have had Robert come with her to meet the family, but given it was her parents' turn to host the family get-together she knew her whole family would be under one roof. She was not concerned about him meeting her parents as much as all the aunts, uncles, and cousins. There were a variety of personalities that was hard to explain to ordinary people. That was why she chose to work in Chicago and not be near them on a daily basis.

"As good as that may sound, I can't do that to my mother. It's her year to host the Christmas open house, the whole family will be over, and I promised to help her."

"Next year we're planning something with just the two of us."

"We will see about that. Right now I won't promise you anything because Christmas has always been a time when my family would get together."

Robert bent over and kissed her gently. What Megan was describing was so unlike his family. Both his parents were only children, so there were never extended families over during the holiday season, only friends from the country club or work.

"I want you to spend Easter with me at my parents in April," Robert whispered.

The look of disappointment on her face went unnoticed by Robert, as she had planned on having him meet her parents over Easter. Now she would have to come up with another time when she could introduce him to her parents. Life was getting complicated.

All she could muster up to say was. "I'll have to check my Franklin Planner."

Robert felt it was an odd comment and wondered why Megan was reluctant to meet his family. He only hoped in time that she would change her mind. If they were ever going to tie the knot then meeting the prospective parents would be a necessity at some point.

* * *

The trees around the apartment complex twinkled with Christmas lights. It was reminiscent of home for Megan, as her father would trim the house and bushes out front with lights and figurines. Megan loved Christmas and all that came with it. As dysfunctional as her family was, it was who she was in the end. But it would be hard to explain to Robert the dynamics in just one meeting with them. It was important to her for him to meet her parents first, and then maybe the extended family sometime in the distant future. Preferably meeting a few at a time, so as not to be too overwhelming.

As they drove up to the compound, Megan put that thought out of her mind. She did not have to deal with it just yet, and when the time came, she would try to explain the complex relationships that made up her relatives. She was fortunate her father was an only child, but that left her mother's side of the family that more than made up for no siblings on her father's side.

Robert parked his BMW next to Megan's Outback and quickly got out to open Megan's door.

Robert knew all the right ways to treat a woman. He was always opening doors for her and helping her on with her coat when they went out. The one task of gallantry he did that surprised her was he always took the outside when walking on a sidewalk and she wondered if they came to a puddle if he would lay down his coat or possibly carry her over the puddle. One thing she was sure of, he would not let her get wet feet.

As the door opened, Robert offered his hand. "I'm going to miss you," he said in slightly above a whisper.

Slowly they walked up the sidewalk to the entrance. Megan wished the evening would last. She was not looking forward to the five days they would be apart, but she did not have it in her to invite him to her parents. She just turned to look up at him.

"Why don't you come up and I'll give you your Christmas gift?" Megan asked.

Robert smiled sheepishly. "I was hoping you would ask."

Megan pointed an accusing finger. "No, you're not spending the night. I have to get up early to catch my flight. I don't need to miss it."

"I could drive you to your parents and save you the plane fare?"

Megan shook her head vehemently. "In time you'll meet them, but not this Christmas."

Robert stopped at the entrance door and pulled Megan into his arms. He kissed her ever so gently on the lips and then whispered, “I love you, Megan Montgomery.”

CHAPTER 4

Megan had not slept well, going over in her head all night the details of last evening's dinner with Robert. Although disappointed that it was not an engagement ring she'd received as a Christmas gift, she was pleasantly pleased with the diamond pendant. She would wear it to her parents' and when she was bombarded with questions about a boyfriend she could flaunt the gift he gave her.

By the time the alarm sounded at five, she was not ready to wake up, but there was no time to sleep in. Her bags were packed, and the taxi already scheduled for a pickup at six. She had an hour to shower and dress and be on her way to the airport. Megan quickly turned on WGN to catch the weather. To her dismay they announced airport delays, which she listened to carefully and her heart sank when the announcer said due to inclement weather anyone leaving O'Hare could expect a forty-five-minute delay. So what else was new, she told herself? She had never flown home where the plane left on time. In the end, she knew she did not have to rush any longer.

Megan leisurely took her shower while listening to Christmas music to get in the mood for the holiday season. For some unknown reason, it had eluded her this year. But as hard as she tried, the prospect of spending time with her family was not really how she wanted to spend the holiday. She walked out of the bathroom wrapped in her towel and glanced at the two bags of gifts along with her luggage. Megan was not sure how she would get them all on the plane, but try she must. It occurred to her it would have been less of a hassle if she had waited until she got home to do her shopping but somehow she had tried desperately to get into the mood and thought maybe shopping for gifts would help.

When the doorman rang up her apartment, she quickly hurried out with her arms laden with her luggage and bags.

* * *

The drive to the airport was nerve-wracking. Although she knew there was going to be a delay, she just did not want to chance missing her flight—knowing full well that holiday bookings made for a full plane and if she by chance missed this flight, there probably would not be another for a few days. She'd promised her mother to come home early so she would be able to help with the preparation for the big family gathering. There would be cookies to bake, and the fixings for a huge turkey dinner. The last time she talked to her mother she'd just purchased a thirty-pound turkey for the event. It was going to be a hectic time, but a time filled with joy helping her mother reminding her of past Christmases growing up. But those Christmases were spent at Nana's, where the open house was always held. This year was the first Christmas without her and the glue that held the family together.

The horns blaring caused Megan to look out the window and realize she was at her destination. Once Megan paid the driver and had her bags on the curb, she quickly grabbed a cart to use to carry her luggage and gifts. She then hurried through the terminal. Holiday travelers lined the various airline counters as Megan rushed to the Northwest ticket counter. She checked in her luggage and then went through security and walked over to the waiting area. Once she got that far, she finally breathed a sigh of relief, knowing full well she was on her way home.

"Northwest Airlines flight 3237 to CWA is boarding at Terminal 2 gate F12," was announced over the loudspeaker.

Megan got up with the other passengers and followed along slowly to the boarding gate. She quickly found her seat and put her carry-on in the overhead luggage bin, thankful that she was able to check the two bags of gifts even though it cost her a little more for the luxury. It was well worth it not having to carry them onto the plane. Megan glanced out the window impatiently as everyone tried to find space in the overhead bins, cramping them to capacity. Megan prayed the plane would not be overloaded and would make it off the tarmac.

Robert slowly entered the plane, following behind everyone. He glanced down the row of seats until his eyes finally rested on the person and the place he was looking for. Megan was too busy looking out the window at the Christmas lights twinkling around the terminal to notice any of the other passengers. Robert slowly maneuvered his way to where she was sitting.

Suddenly someone stood in front of Megan's seat. She did not look up and only hoped it was not one of those friendly people who would tell you their life story in the thirty-five minutes it would take them to fly to CWA in central Wisconsin. Robert cleared his throat as Megan finally glanced up. She leaned back and stared up at Robert for the longest time without saying a word. Finally, she gained her composure.

"What are you doing here?" she snapped.

One part of her was happy to see him, but there was the other side that realized the awkwardness of the situation.

"Catching my flight," Robert said with a big grin on his face.

"What?" Megan almost choked on the word.

"I wanted to spend Christmas with you," he said as he reached up and stuffed his carry-on in the last remaining space. He then sat down next to Megan. "I was tired of waiting for you to ask so when you didn't, I decided to come on my own."

"But we agreed," she argued.

"No. You agreed. I just didn't argue," he countered.

Megan shook her head. "You can't be serious. You have to get off the plane."

Robert handed Megan his ticket. She examined it hoping above all else that this was a sick joke, but his ticket read the same as hers did. He, too, was flying to CWA. She blinked a few times hoping that by doing so she could will the destination to be someplace else, any place else but CWA. She just was not prepared for him to meet her family just yet, but then she had no choice in the matter now.

Robert leaned over and kissed her on the cheek. "Relax, we'll have fun."

"You have no clue what you are in for."

"Well, give me a hint."

"My parents are the only normal ones in the family," Megan said and then thought a moment. "Oh yeah, except for my aunts Carrie and Susan."

"What's wrong with the rest?"

Megan laughed while shaking her head. "Aunt Judy, oh I can't even begin to explain her, and..." Megan stopped a moment as she sighed deeply. "What's the use? You'll just have to meet them all and make your judgment of them. Just promise me you won't hate me after this holiday."

Robert took hold of Megan's hand and kissed it for reassurance. At that moment he was more concerned about what Megan would think about his parents, not about her side of the family.

"I promise I'll still love you."

The stewardess quickly went through the safety instructions while Robert held onto Megan's hand. It was a gesture to make her more at ease about him coming home with her.

* * *

Snow was falling by the time the plane landed at CWA. It was truly going to be a white Christmas. Robert was the first one down the aircraft steps, followed closely by Megan. She took a deep breath and was thankful that she told her parents not to meet her at the airport, that she would be renting a car for her stay. It would at least give her a little more time to adjust to the fact that Robert was with her.

They quickly walked into the terminal and followed other passengers to the luggage carousel. Robert had the one bag while Megan had the two bags of presents and the one suitcase, along with the carry-on that she had on the plane.

Robert turned to her. "How long were you planning on being here?"

"I told you, five days. I can't very well cut it short now. My parents have things planned. We do this whole tradition thing."

"I didn't know how to prepare for the weather. So I think I over packed, so I came prepared."

When Robert saw the two bags of gifts, he turned to Megan. "I didn't bring presents. Will you help me go shopping, so I at least have gifts for your parents?"

"You don't have to."

"Trust me, I do," Robert quickly added.

All the planning he did for this surprise, it completely slipped his mind about Megan's parents and the imposition he was putting on them by surprising them with an additional guest for a holiday. He was not going to impose on them and not at least be courteous enough to remember them at Christmas. Especially seeing he was going to ask for their daughter's hand in marriage. What kind of impression would that leave?

Once they had their luggage, Robert walked over to the Hertz rental car counter. The only car left was a small Honda Civic, and that would have to do. Megan handed Robert the keys.

"Do you want to drive?"

"You know the way, you drive."

"I'll drop you off at the hotel."

Robert glanced at his watch. "It's too early for check-in. I'll go with you to your parents first."

Megan looked at him as panic set in. There was no way out of the situation. She might as well get it over with and the sooner, the better as far as she was concerned. When the introduction to her parents was over with, she would have plenty of time to explain to them why she never mentioned she had been dating Robert for almost a year.

Once they were in the car, Megan tried to relax, but she could not convince herself that all would go well. She sat behind the wheel clutched it tightly and just took a deep breath. Her knuckles turned white as she drove down the highway. It did not take long, and she turned off the exit and drove down winding roads until they came to the neighborhood of her birth. Megan turned to Robert.

"Here we are," she said, pulling into the driveway of a lovely two-story colonial style house with an attached three-car garage. All the houses in the neighborhood were similar in build with large back yards. It was typical upper middle class.

Robert turned to her and smiled while taking her hand and patting it for reassurance. “Relax,” he said softly.

“Easy for you to say.”

Robert laughed as he opened the door and got out. Megan popped the trunk while Robert quickly walked to the back and took out Megan’s luggage along with the two shopping bags of gifts. The front door opened just then. Sara, Megan’s mother, an attractive gray-haired, perpetually cheerful woman, rushed out to greet them. She was wearing a bright red Christmas sweater with twinkling lights. When she saw Megan, she rushed up to hug her daughter and kiss her on the cheek.

“I’m so glad you’re finally here,” Sara said.

“I was here just a month ago for Josh’s wedding.”

Sara looked at Megan. “That was just one day, and you were in and out with no time to visit.”

Sara glanced over at Robert curiously, then turned back to Megan and mouthed, “Who is your friend?”

“Oh, mom, I’d like you to meet Robert. I told you about him,” Megan said as she looked at her mom in a way that told her to go along with it.

Sara in turn just stared at Robert. She looked him up and down and was impressed by what she saw. But she still appeared puzzled by Megan trying to convince her that she had told her about him.

“No. I don’t think you ever mentioned him. I think I would have remembered it.”

Robert sensed the discomfort that Megan was in and stepped forward. “Glad to meet you finally.”

Sara whispered, “Finally?” She turned to the garage as if looking for someone or something. “Ben,” she yelled.

Megan's father slowly walked out of the garage, while struggling to carry a big box of Christmas lights.

Ben's gray hair could be seen tucked under the stocking cap, he had a youthful face with mischievous eyes. When he saw Megan he quickly set the box down and hurried over.

"Daddy," Megan said running up to her father and jumped into his arms.

"Ben, this is Megan's friend," Sara said it in a way that kind of indicated she was still a little puzzled.

Ben released one arm from around Megan and extended it to Robert while also giving him the once-over.

"I have to drop him off at the Holiday Inn," Megan said.

"Oh no, he can stay here. There's plenty of room."

Megan quickly replied, "We don't want to impose on you."

But Ben cut her off quickly. "We don't have Sara's mother this year, so we have plenty of room."

Robert smiled pleasantly at Megan before he looked at Ben. "I'd love to spend Christmas with you."

Megan just stared at Robert. The look she gave him a clear indication she was not happy with the situation. But this was exactly what he wanted, to spend time with her parents and get to know Megan's family. She had been putting him off long enough.

Ben turned to Megan. "Show him the spare bedroom, and then after he's unpacked Robert can help me with the Christmas lights."

Robert followed Megan into the house. He knew she was not happy with him, but in time he hoped she would see this was for the best. It was only a matter of time that he would have to meet her family and why not now? She would understand it all once he asked her father for her hand in marriage. For him, things were working out as planned.

Once they were out of sight of her parents and they were upstairs walking down the hallway to the bedrooms, Megan finally turned to Robert.

"You planned this all along, didn't you?"

"Not staying here, if that's what you mean," Robert said in his defense.

They reached the spare bedroom. Megan looked up at Robert and just shook her head after opening the door.

"Here you go," she pointed. "The bathroom is down the hall to your right."

"There's no bathroom off the bedroom?" Robert asked and then wished he had bit his tongue after saying the words.

Megan laughed. "This isn't the Ritz."

"I didn't mean it that way," he said.

"You better hurry, Daddy doesn't like to be kept waiting."

"What are you going to do," Robert asked.

"I'm sure mom is busy in the kitchen baking cookies. I'll just help her. But I'd like to go shopping later if you don't mind."

"I'll go with you. I'd like to get something for your parents."

"As I said, you don't have to do that."

Robert knew he did not have to, but if he wanted to ask Megan to marry him, it was almost a must. Plus he wanted to leave the impression of being a dutiful suitor, one worthy of their daughter. And the fact that they were putting him up for a holiday made it now a must do situation.

"Trust me, Megan, it's the least I can do. Besides, I didn't expect them to put me up for a holiday."

It was going to be an interesting weekend. So far he liked Ben, who was unlike his uptight father. And Sara doing her holiday baking was so unlike his mother, who never stepped foot in the kitchen except to complain that the steak was overcooked. And her idea of cooking was meeting the bakery chef and personally picking out the assortment of Christmas fare she planned to purchase. But Robert figured that task was left up to the kitchen staff.

CHAPTER 5

Megan was busy with Sara, first making the cutout cookies and then later decorating them. Sara frosted the cookies while Megan decorated them with colored sugars and sprinkles. She spent extra time on the cut out Christmas trees, putting silver balls and cinnamon hearts on the tips. Megan glanced out the side window at Robert and Ben hanging the lights and candy canes on the fence along the driveway. Once done with that they got the step ladder out and hung the icicle lights on the garage eaves and spread multicolored lights on all the shrubs and trees in the front yard. The weather was warm outside even though light snowflakes fell, making for a fitting day to hang lights. It was something Ben should have had done weeks earlier but procrastinated doing it until now.

"Robert seems like a nice young man," Sara said as she watched Ben and Robert hang yet another string of lights.

"He is," was all Megan could say. She now regretted not being honest with her mother about her relationship with Robert. There had been plenty of time this past year to tell her about him. But she didn't want to jinx it for fear it wouldn't last.

"How long have you two been an item?"

"Is it that obvious?"

"We wouldn't have invited him to stay if we didn't think you two had been dating," Sara said and then quickly added, "You know you can be honest with us."

"I know, Mom."

"Why didn't you bring him to Josh's wedding last month?"

"I would have, but the invitation was only for me, and not extended to a friend."

"Judy made such a production out of your not having a date." Sara looked puzzled.

"Honestly, Mom, Aunt Judy was probably playing one of her games again. The invitation was only for me. I wasn't going to bring Robert when clearly a friend was not included on my invitation."

"Oh well, what goes around, comes around."

Robert and Ben walked in. Ben grabbed one of the decorated cookies and quickly ate it.

"Best damn Christmas cookies in town. Robert, you can take one too."

Robert glanced at Megan as if to ask if it was okay and then reached for one of the big Christmas tree cookies. He took a bite and had never experienced his jaw muscles aching, because of something that was so delicious.

Sara opened the cupboard and took out two glasses and then poured some milk for the men. It was the perfect complement to a fresh-baked cookie.

"You guys finished with hanging the lights?"

Ben gulped the milk and then quickly added with frustration, "Yeah, we ran out of lights."

Sara turned to Robert. "Every year he picks up more lights at the end of the year sales and every year he still runs out. I swear one of these years he'll have enough so the space station can see our house."

Ben bent down and kissed Sara on the neck in a gesture of love.

"Oh, you are cold," she said, wrapping her arms around herself to take the chill away.

"Robert and I are going to go out and cut down our Christmas tree before you guys go shopping."

Robert turned to Ben. "Don't you just go out and buy one?"

Ben looked at Robert and laughed. "What's the fun in that?" he said, turning to Megan as if saying, "Where did you get this guy?"

Sara just turned to Megan and then looked at Robert. "Keep in mind we have ten-foot ceilings in the living room, and I'd like it in the corner. I don't like it too wide at the bottom."

Ben just shook his head and laughed. But the look on Sara's face was a clear indication that she was serious.

"I've been doing this for thirty-five years and had I ever come home with something we couldn't use?"

Sara looked at Ben and was about to say something. Ben pointed the finger at her. "Don't answer that."

* * *

Ben took Robert for a ride around town, stopping at a few tree lots, but Ben was unable to find the perfect tree. It was not until they drove further up north when they saw the 'Cut Your Own Tree' sign. Ben drove up the long driveway and parked the car alongside the other cars, and they quickly got out. Ben took the saw out of the trunk and started walking down the long rows of blue spruce trees. They walked around the tree farm looking at the beautifully trimmed trees for nearly an hour, and then suddenly in the distance, Ben spied the tree he was looking for. It stood a good sixteen feet tall and stuck out from all the rest because of its perfect shape and the tallness of its size. Ben was in awe of the tree.

All Robert could do was just stand there with his mouth open. He just stared up at the tree, not believing this was the one Ben wanted. He kept thinking of Sara's instructions and wondered what she would say when she saw the tree.

"Ben, I think this tree is too tall," Robert finally said, trying to be diplomatic about the situation so as not to hurt Ben's ego.

"What do you mean? It's perfect," Ben argued.

Robert just shook his head. He raised his hand and knew that the tree should not be much taller than a foot beyond the tip of his finger for it to fit in the space Sara had in mind. Besides, the base had to be at least ten feet across. Robert stepped back to get a better look and, looking at it next to Ben, he was positive once they got home they would be in trouble with Sara.

"Ben, I think we should rethink this tree," Robert said with a pleading look on his face. He only hoped Ben would take a good look at the tree and agree with him.

Ben laughed mockingly. "Ridiculous. It will fit perfectly."

Robert's eyes popped out while Ben stepped back and with open arms smiled broadly. In an Italian accent, he quickly announced. "It's a nice-a-tree,"

"Didn't your wife say the living room has a ten-foot ceiling?"

Ben just looked at Robert and shook his head. "Hey, it's perfect." As if by saying it, he made it so.

Robert looked puzzled as he stared up at the Christmas tree while Ben took out the saw and crawled under the bottom of the tree and started sawing away.

* * *

The tree was tied to the top of Ben's car. The trunk of the tree stuck out four feet in front of the car hood while the top hung out a good three feet off the back.

As they passed cars people stared at the huge Christmas tree. It embarrassed Robert watching passengers in these cars laughing at them.

Slowly the car pulled into the driveway. Ben had a proud look on his face, but before the car could come to a complete halt, Sara was already running out of the house. She appeared in shock when she saw the tree. Megan hurried out after her. She had her coat and purse in hand. As soon as Robert got out of the car, she dragged him off.

“Mom, if you don’t mind, Robert and I are going shopping,” she quickly spouted out without waiting for a reply.

Robert just turned to Sara and held up his hands while shaking his head. He looked pathetically helpless.

“Maybe we should stay,” Robert turned to Megan and whispered, knowing full well that Ben was in trouble and figured with them there, the wrath of Sara might not be so bad.

Megan cut in. “We are leaving. Trust me. You don’t want to be around for this.”

Sara stood with her hands on her hips and just glared at Ben. Finally, she turned to Megan and Robert and pointed. “Go,” Sara said. “I think your father and I have to have a little talk.”

Megan grabbed Robert by the sleeve. He looked at Ben helplessly. Ben appeared like a man who knew what was to come as he looked at the tree and finally realized just how big it was.

When they walked halfway down the driveway, Megan turned to Robert. “What were you thinking?”

Robert just shook his head. “It wasn’t my fault. He wouldn’t listen.”

Megan quickly got into the car while Robert hopped into the passenger seat before Megan could take off without him. He too actually did not want to be around when Ben tried to get the tree into the house.

* * *

The mall was filled with Christmas shoppers while "Deck the Halls" played on a continual loop in the background to get everyone into the holiday spirit. Megan only had a few more people to buy for, while Robert was having the most trouble trying to find something appropriate for Megan's parents. He did not want to appear too pretentious yet wanted to impress them. And given Megan's mood about the tree, she was being no help in getting him out of trouble with Sara.

Josh, Megan's cousin, and his new very pregnant wife, Sandy, walked up behind the two shoppers.

"Hello, stranger," Josh said.

Megan turned. She looked at Josh and could not help looking at Sandy. She was laden down with bags filled with wrapped gifts, but it did nothing to hide the fact she was pregnant.

Megan reached over and kissed her cousin on the cheek. "Cuz," she said, her favorite term of endearment for him. She turned again to Sandy and then looked at Josh. "Boy, you move fast."

Josh just laughed as he glanced at Robert. "Who's your friend?"

"Oh, Robert, this is my cousin Josh and his wife, Sandy."

Robert extended a hand to Josh and then glanced at Sandy's protruding belly.

"So, when are you due?"

Sandy set the bags down and then rubbed her belly. "End of January. Maybe we'll have a Super Bowl baby?"

"Not on your life," Josh piped in. "That day is already taken and I ain't missing the game for no baby."

Megan frowned at what Josh had just said. In all reality, he could very easily tape the game and catch it later if the baby chose that day to come.

“Maybe a Valentine baby?” Megan said, trying to defuse the remark.

“Now I could deal with that,” Sandy replied. “But that would add a few weeks more to carrying this little bundle of joy.” She said it in a way you knew she was not enjoying the carry-on luggage onboard.

“It would save me a gift,” Josh said.

“Oh no, it wouldn’t. I’d expect something even bigger.”

“Well, then a Super Bowl baby it better be.”

Sandy winced a little as if in pain. It went unnoticed by the two men, but not Megan.

“You okay?” Megan asked.

“Oh yeah. The baby has been resting on a nerve that’s killing me at times.”

Megan turned to Josh and frowned. “It probably doesn’t help carrying all those bags.”

Josh took the hint and bent down and picked up a few of the bags. Sandy smiled at Megan and mouthed a big “thank you.”

“We were just on our way out to the car anyway.”

Megan turned to Josh. “So did Uncle Jake make it in?”

“Yeah, he wouldn’t miss Christmas in Wisconsin for nothing,” he said and then turned to Robert. “Maybe you’d like to go ice fishing with us guys tomorrow. Our annual tradition.”

Megan panicked a moment but tried to hide her apprehension given the excitement on Robert’s face at meeting more of her family.

“Uh...” Megan said, unable to come up with an excuse, but Robert cut her off quickly.

“Sure. I’ll have to get a license though.”

Josh turned to Megan and smiled. “I’ll call you later and we can discuss the details. Don’t worry about clothes. I’m sure Ben will lend you some of his from his snowmobiling days. Besides, we spend a lot of time in our vehicles."

Josh and Sandy walked off leaving Robert to watch them for a moment. Robert turned to Megan and smiled.

"Isn't that the wedding you went to last month?"

"Yeah," was all Megan could muster up to reply. She didn't want to say anything more than that for fear Robert would wonder why she did not have him come with her.

Robert shrugged and then just uttered an understanding "oh."

Robert took Megan's hand as they continued on with their shopping. There was no time to waste, as this would be the only shopping trip out for him before Christmas. He was enjoying meeting various members of Megan's family. They all seemed so friendly and close. He wondered why Megan was so apprehensive about him being there.

CHAPTER 6

Robert and Megan spent another hour shopping at the mall. With the help of Megan, Robert finally found an appropriate gift for her parents at a little crystal shop near the entrance. It was the Waterford Irish Lace bowl that caught Robert's attention when he remembered Megan telling him once about her parents' Waterford collection. He knew it would be a nice addition to their current collection and an appropriate gift from a future son-in-law.

Megan and Robert laughed when entering the driveway. The seven-foot trunk from the Christmas tree her father brought home earlier rested on top of the snow bank for garbage pickup in the morning. Megan just shook her head.

"I can't believe you couldn't talk him out of bringing that monstrosity home."

"Hey, he's your father."

"Next time take a tape measure with you."

"Hey, in my defense I stood next to the tree and raised my hand over my head. I knew the tree shouldn't be more than a foot over the tip of my finger. Do you think he would listen? No. He wanted that tree, and there was no changing his mind."

All Megan managed to say as she turned around to walk into the house, was. "Men!"

By the time they entered the house, the table was set for dinner and the meal almost ready. There was just enough time to wash before dinner was served in the dining room and once seated, it was finally time to relax.

Sara had on another Christmas sweater, this one bright red with a Christmas tree down the front and twinkling lights. With her gray hair, the sweater was quite becoming. In the dim light of the dining room, the twinkle of lights was all one could see. On the other hand, Ben's reindeer sweater with bells dangling from the antlers looked a little ridiculous on a man of his stature. One would guess he only wore it to please his wife, especially after the fiasco of the Christmas tree.

"So, Robert, what do you think of our little town?" Ben asked as the reindeer bells jingled.

Robert has a hard time keeping a straight face and finally gained control. "It's not so little. The mall was quite impressive."

"I figure you'd end up there."

"It wasn't that crowded. Besides, I still had a few things to pick up," Megan remarked as she turned to Sara. She could tell that the tension about the tree had passed.

"We met Josh and his wife," Robert said trying to stay in the conversation.

Megan passed the potatoes to Robert and then turned back to her mother.

"I was going to ask you, whatever happened to Jill? Wasn't that Memorial Day that everyone expected Josh to give her a ring?"

"That's a story in itself," Ben piped in with a big grin on his face.

"Ben," Sara snapped in a way that indicated it was a subject not to be discussed over dinner. She quickly turned to Megan. "They obviously broke up."

Megan stood up and walked into the kitchen and grabbed the coffee pot off the kitchen counter and hurried back into the dining room. She quickly topped off everyone's coffee cup and then set the pot on the hot plate on the table. Once done, she turned to her mother.

"So what happened?" Megan asked.

Sara just sighed while she shook her head. Avoiding the subject was useless. "Jill's mother told me Josh broke up because he wanted to sow his wild oats."

"He should have prayed for a crop failure on Sunday," Ben laughed uncontrollably.

Robert choked on his food while Megan quickly patted him on the back. She too was having a hard time not finding humor in the situation.

"Do they know what they are having?"

"A girl, I think," Sara added.

"It would be poetic justice for him to have about three girls all total," Ben laughed.

Ben enjoyed the conversation, especially when it came to Sara's family. There was always an array of topics to discuss and there was always never-ending drama when it came to one of Sara's sisters.

"Yeah, I would love to be a fly on the wall when he tries to explain to his daughters about saving themselves for their husbands."

The doorbell rang, startling those at the table. Sara was relieved for the interruption as she quickly got up and hurried to the front door.

"I wonder who that could be," she said as she disappeared. The back of the sweater was adorned with a wreath with twinkling lights.

Robert had a hard time keeping his eyes off the sweater. Megan kicked him from under the table, startling him for an instant, and then he looked at her and saw the frown on her face. In all actuality, Megan's parents were normal in every way, but their holiday attire.

Sara opened the door and there, with reindeer antlers clipped to his hat, was Jake, Sara's younger brother. The family resemblance was unmistakable. The only difference was his blue eyes were blood-shot, and he reeked of pot. Sara fanned the air, as there was still a cloud of smoke from the joint he just put out.

"How's my favorite sister?" he said as he grabbed Sara and hoisted her up off her feet.

"You say that to all your sisters." Sara quickly pushed him away once Jake released her, not wanting the smell of pot to cling to her sweater.

Ben walked up behind Sara and glanced suspiciously at Jake's bloodshot eyes but said nothing. It was not the time or the place given they had company in the house and Ben did not want to embarrass Megan or her friend by dealing with Jake's problem just then. The family tended to ignore the situation hoping, in the end, it would just go away, but in time the problem had only gotten worse. Ben feared that this just might be the year the family would finally have to deal with Jake's habit because it was affecting other family members.

"I wasn't sure you'd make it back given you were just home last month."

"Wouldn't be Christmas without coming home."

Megan and Robert walked out of the dining room. When Megan heard Jake's voice, she wanted Robert to meet her uncle. Once Megan saw Jake and his bloodshot eyes, she regretted coming to the door.

Megan leaned over to her father and whispered, "He probably had a shipment that had to be delivered."

Megan could have bitten her tongue when she realized that Robert also heard what she said. Megan only hoped that Robert would not want an explanation.

"He's a trucker?" Robert asked.

Megan was embarrassed, and all she could say was. "No, it's nothing like that."

Once Robert got a whiff of Uncle Jake and quickly understood the flip remark Megan made and just stepped back. He had been around enough college buddies to know what pot smelled like.

"Won't you come in and sit down with us? I'll set another plate," Sara said ignoring the reluctant look that Ben gave her just then.

Uncle Jake was placed next to Robert, who found it hard to come up with anything to say to Jake. He understood what shipment Megan was talking about now, and realized Megan's mood change. It was one of those dirty little family secrets that everyone knew about but refused to discuss openly.

Once the meal was over with, Sara and Megan quickly cleared off the table. Ben appeared moody and just got up and walked into his den and closed the door, a clear indication he wanted to be alone. Jake got up and followed the women into the kitchen and then turned to Sara.

"I think I'll get a little fresh air," he said. Without waiting for a reply, he walked out of the kitchen door and stood on the back porch.

Once the door was shut, Megan turned to her mother. Sara was busy running water for the dishes and pretended not to notice Megan watching her. Finally, Megan shut the water off, turned to her mother to get her attention.

"I can't believe he came after what happened at Josh's wedding," Megan snapped.

Jake had almost gotten Josh arrested by the prank he pulled. It was only by luck that Ben stepped in before the police came and were able to remove the dining hall of the bags of pot Jake gave Josh as a wedding gift.

"Ben never had much tolerance for Jake."

"Do you blame him? There was Josh's wedding and not to mention the crap he pulled after Nana died."

"I don't want to go there," Sara snapped. "It's Christmas, let's just get along."

Robert walked in from the dining room carrying a load of dishes. He was a little uneasy when he realized he'd walked in on an argument between the two women. Megan motioned to the door and mouthed, "Go outside." Robert took his cue and walked over to the kitchen door and stepped out onto the porch. To his surprise, Jake was smoking a joint. Robert didn't know what to do. A part of him wanted to go back into the house and call the cops, but this was Megan's uncle. And calling the cops on a relative was not a good first impression for the rest of the family.

Jake just smiled at Robert and took another drag on the joint. He handed it to Robert, but Robert just raised his hand in refusal.

"How long have you been screwing my niece?" Jake asked jokingly.

Robert choked. "What?" is all he could muster up to say given how crude the remark was.

"I'm joking. You can take a joke, can't you?"

Robert just shook his head, not believing what he had just heard.

"I better get back in there," Robert quickly said and then hesitated a moment. "It's cold out here."

Jake crushed the joint and then bent down and picked up the butt and put it in his shirt pocket.

"I got to leave anyway," he replied and then turned to Robert. "Tell Sara I'll see her tomorrow."

Robert turned. Before he walked back into the kitchen, he quickly fanned the air. Sara was standing at the sink alone.

"Where's Megan?" Robert asked.

"Oh, she had a headache. I sent her upstairs."

Ben walked in and looked at Robert. "Where is Jake?"

"He left and said he would see you guys tomorrow."

Ben looked at Sara for the longest time, and Robert sensed they wanted to be alone. It was evident there was an undercurrent of discontentment about Jake's visit. So Robert just walked out of the room. He knew this was going to be a difficult situation and did not want to stick around for what was to come.

When Ben thought Robert was out of earshot, he went up to Sara, who by then was upset. She had just spent the last few minutes arguing with her daughter about a problem that the family had chosen to ignore for years.

"I swear I'll report him. I don't want him doing his drugs on my property." Ben snapped.

"It's for medical purposes."

Ben pointed his finger at Sara. "I don't care what excuse he gives you."

"I'll talk to him," was all Sara could muster up to say.

Jake in all actuality wasn't suffering from anything that was clinically diagnosed. The family always made excuses for his usage of pot for medical purposes, but now that he'd gotten Josh involved, this was becoming a dangerous situation.

CHAPTER 7

Megan was walking out of the bathroom when Robert walked up the stairs. She looked at Robert and could see the troubled look on his face.

"I was wondering where you were off to."

"I was with Jake on the porch. Do you know what he smokes?"

"You didn't?" Megan asked.

"No."

"Did mom or dad see him?"

"I don't think so, but then you couldn't miss the smell. And just because they didn't see Jake, doesn't mean they don't know."

"Oh shit, that's all I need is a family fight," Megan said as she walked into her bedroom and sat down on the bed.

Robert just stood in the doorway. He looked at Megan for the longest time. "Everyone seems to know about his problem? It's like the elephant in the room, pretending it isn't there doesn't make it so."

Megan nodded as she looked up at Robert. Tears welled up in her eyes as she fought the urge to cry.

"Now you know why I didn't want you here."

"That's no big thing. I'll just stay away from him."

"It ain't that easy," Megan said.

"Just relax. So far things have gone okay. What's the worst thing that could happen?"

"You haven't met the rest of the family yet."

Robert walked over to Megan and sat down next to her. He took her hands in his and kissed them while trying to reassure her.

He whispered in her ear. "Once you've met my family we'll compare notes on dysfunction," he said. "Now how is your headache?"

Megan looked up at him, sensing he only said that to make her feel better. She leaned her head into him. It was then she knew why she loved him so much and regretted not introducing him sooner to her parents. At least it would have made meeting the rest of the family in the next few days a little less traumatic.

* * *

Once the fiasco of Uncle Jake's visit was behind them, Robert and Megan went downstairs and joined her parents in the living room. Both still had on their holiday sweaters. The music that played in the background put everyone back into a holiday mood. Sara quickly walked into the kitchen and was back in a flash. She had a big smile as she served up the rum-spiked apple cider in reindeer mugs with a cinnamon stick in each for added flavor.

Robert drank half of his when he started feeling its effect. Ben got up and walked over to the fireplace and stoked the fire. There was something about the wood heat that warmed a person's inner core.

To Robert, this whole experience was unlike his past holidays with his parents. The Christmas music was playing in the background, and the old-fashioned lights were twinkling brightly with candy ornaments that were scattered around the tree all added to the mystic of the festive occasion. Even though he was new to their tradition, it excited him seeing all the gifts stacked as high as the bottom branches and went all around the tree. Secretly, like when he was a child, he hoped a few were for him.

He laughed to himself thinking about the flocked tree with the coordinated glass balls that matched the color scheme of the house. His mother never allowed gifts under the tree, as she thought that was tacky. As far back as he could remember it was always a bank card for him to pick out something he wanted at any store he chose. Somehow this was more exciting. Not knowing what was in those colorfully wrapped presents brought out the little boy in him.

Ben had been silent for the longest time. He watched Robert, as he could not take his eyes off the tree or the gifts underneath the tree.

“So, Megan tells me you’re going fishing with Josh in the morning?” Ben asked.

“Yeah, I guess Jake and an Uncle Johnny are coming too.”

Robert relayed this in a way that showed he was a little hesitant at spending any time with Uncle Jake given what happened earlier that evening. But Robert decided to be both gracious and cautious in the time he spent with Jake. He was not taking any chances and knew now he would have to be ever on his guard.

Ben laughed. “The Three Stooges.”

Sara looked sternly at Ben. “Ben, now that isn’t very nice.”

“Would you rather have me say Dumb, Dumber, and Dumbest?”

Robert turned to Megan and then looked at Ben with concern on his face. “It can’t be that bad.”

“Well, when Jake and Josh get together that’s a perfect mix for trouble following soon. Then you throw in

Uncle Johnny and," Ben hesitated and then just shook his head, "disaster is in the works for sure."

Robert gulped the apple cider. He had a strong feeling he would need it to calm his nerves about spending time with Uncle Jake tomorrow. He had met Josh, and he seemed normal enough. Robert only hoped that things were not as bad as Ben was making them out to be. But then Ben had been in the family for years now and knew everyone's little quirks. Robert had yet to meet Uncle Johnny. He only wished not to have any unforeseen disaster happen and hoped the day ran smoothly.

Sara cleared her throat and then gave Ben a warning glance that was a clear indication to stop that line of talk. She finally turned to Robert.

"How do your parents spend the holidays?"

Robert appeared a little embarrassed and tried desperately to think of something appropriate to say so as not to put on airs with Megan's parents. He found it hard to say they were traveling around Europe for the holiday season.

Megan, sensing Robert's discomfort, quickly piped in. "They probably do the same things we do, Mom."

"I suppose your mother bakes cookies as I do?"

Robert shrugged. "The cook does that. But I think the cook just orders them from a bakery because I've never seen her work in the kitchen like what you and Megan were doing earlier."

"That's sad," Sara said, looking a little concerned. "Won't they miss seeing you over the holiday?"

"They have done this every year since I was in college. So I'm used to being on my own over the holidays."

"Oh," is all Sara could muster up to say.

Ben looked at Robert. "What about the Christmas lights? You knew what to do this afternoon."

"I used to help the caretaker decorate. My father was always too busy to be bothered with that. Plus, I don't think he would know the first thing to do when it comes to decorating the outside, let alone open up a step ladder."

"That is too bad. I'm a hands-on kind of guy. I only let someone do what I know nothing about," Ben said with pride.

Sara looked at him and laughed. "Maybe next year you should hire someone to pick out our Christmas tree. At least we will not have to cut off half the tree to fit it in the house."

Ben's face turned red at the remark, but he said nothing in his defense. He knew full well this was not an argument he could ever win.

Robert just shrugged. Up until then he never really gave it a thought. But after spending the morning helping Ben with the decorations outside, Robert realized just how much he missed doing things like that with his father. It never really was the same when he worked with the caretaker, although he and Hank always got along. Robert drank the last of the apple cider and then quickly poured more into his glass.

Robert turned to Megan with excitement in his eyes. "You know there was something I always wanted to do at Christmas time."

"What's that, pray tell?" she asked reluctantly.

"Go Christmas caroling."

Megan looked at him with raised eyebrows as if not believing what he had just said. "You are kidding, aren't you?"

"No. I'm serious."

Sara glanced at Ben and then turned to Robert and Megan. "Why not? It would be fun. We could go in the next subdivision where people do not know us," she quickly added.

Sara promptly got out her Christmas songbooks. Although she knew most of the songs by heart, it was always easier when you had the book in hand. Plus, Sara was not sure how well Robert knew all the Christmas songs, and if he were anything like Ben, he would need the songbook in front of him. Sara quickly handed Megan and Robert the songbooks and then followed Ben outside to the car.

* * *

Ben drove to the next subdivision over and parked his car near a vacant lot. The four got out and slowly started their trek up to the first house. Sara had brought red and green candles from home to add to the Christmas spirit rather than flashlights. Ben took out his grill lighter from his jacket pocket and lit the candles. They were all dressed in heavy winter coats with warm hats and mittens, but still, the cold night air seeped through. Ben brought his Christmas bells, so he jingled them while they slowly walked up to the first house on the block.

They stopped for a brief moment before walking up to the front door of the first house. Ben rang the doorbell, and they quickly started to sing, "O come all ye faithful. Joyful and triumphant, O come ye, O come ye to Bethlehem." Before they got to the next verse, the door swung open and a man in a dirty T-shirt with a can of beer in his right hand stood to stare at the group.

"I'm not buying anything you're selling," he said and then slammed the door shut on them.

The man's demeanor surprised Robert, but the rudeness did not sway Sara and she quickly guided the group to the next house.

Sara turned to the other three with a big smile. "Let's just stand here on the sidewalk and sing. Once we are done, we will just walk down the street singing. This way we won't disturb anyone or make them angry," she said cheerfully.

It was as if Sara believed what she had said. Or possibly the rum cider was finally affecting her.

They got through the first verse and started the second verse without a hitch. "Come and behold him, born the king of angels. O come let us adore him, O come let us adore him. O come let us adore him, Christ the Lord."

And all was going well, but no one in the house seemed the least bit curious about the group outside singing. Sara motioned for the group to follow her to the next house down the street. They all appeared to be into singing by then. Even Ben belted out the song, though out of tune. Robert was especially in the musical mood, and his voice seemed to sound louder than the other three. They slowly came to a house that was fenced in, and they stopped at the gate. Sara started singing again, followed by the rest.

"We wish you a Merry Christmas. We wish you a Merry Christmas. We wish you a Merry Christmas, and a Happy New Year. We all know that Santa's coming. We all know that Santa's coming. We all know that Santa's coming and soon will be here."

As they finished the verse the front door opened, but instead of its occupants coming out to offer cookies and hot cider like you see in the movies, a Doberman came rushing out, barking startling the group. They dropped their candles and ran down the street to where the car was parked. By the time they got into the car and pulled out of the neighborhood, a squad car with lights and sirens blaring turned onto the street they'd just left. Robert turned to Megan and burst out laughing.

"That was close."

"I can't believe they called the cops," Megan laughed, almost out of breath.

Ben just looked into the backseat at Robert. "Any more brilliant ideas?"

Robert raised his hands and shook his head. He couldn't stop laughing. Megan turned and put her head on his shoulder and patted him on the chest.

CHAPTER 8

Once Ben pulled into the driveway all four quickly got out of the car and hurried into the house. It was not until they were resting in the living room that Megan sat back on the couch and finally caught her breath. They all exchanged glances and then burst out laughing again. No one could stop laughing about the fiasco of Christmas caroling. It was something they would not be doing again anytime soon.

Megan pointed to Robert. “Not a good idea.”

In the distance, sirens could still be heard and seemed to be getting closer. Who would have thought the simple act of Christmas caroling would have brought out the police in full force?

“Did you see that dog? I thought it would jump the fence. I nearly crapped my pants,” Ben said putting his hand to his heart. “It’s a good thing I don’t have a heart condition because I think we would be making a run to the hospital tonight,” he remarked and then turned to Robert. “And not to go Christmas caroling either.”

Sara took off her jacket and hat and hung them in the hall closet. “I’ll make some hot apple cider.”

By the time Sara walked back out of the kitchen with the tray of four reindeer glasses of apple cider filled to the brim and cinnamon sticks sticking out of each, there was the knock at the front door. Ben glanced out the front window and saw the squad car sitting out front of the house. Sara turned to see what Ben was looking at and noticed the lights flashing of the squad. She set the tray down and took a quick drink of the cider. She turned to the three sitting like little angels in the living room and motioned for them to stay seated.

"I don't want to answer this," she said but knew she had to.

Sara was sure the officers could see that someone was home, so she bit the bullet and walked over to the front door and opened it slowly.

Robert quickly got up and picked up the tray of apple cider, but when he saw the one officer holding two green candles his face turned white. He glanced down at his right hand with the dry green wax droplets on his index finger. He quickly set the tray back down and put his hand behind his back and quickly peeled off the wax with his other hand. Robert then moved forward to support Sara in talking to the officers. He extended his right hand to the officer nearest him. The uniformed officer stood staunchly erect and hesitated a moment before accepting Roberts' hand.

Sara was too tongue-tied to say anything, and Robert feared she would confess to everything. But in all actuality, all they were guilty of doing that night was Christmas caroling. And he did not think there was a law against that. At least not on the books.

"Is there something we can do for you, officers?" Robert said with an innocent look on his face. He turned and saw the relief on Sara's face and knew she was not willing to deal with the officers no matter how innocent she was.

"We had a complaint about strange people running around a few blocks down."

The other officer stepped forward. "They were followed to this neighborhood."

Robert turned to Ben and Megan still sitting in the living room, looking as innocent as ever.

"They dropped these," the one officer said, holding up the green candles.

On the mantel, there were matching green candles that Robert hoped the officers would not notice.

Robert put his hand behind his back for fear he had not peeled all the wax off and turned back to Ben. "Did you see anything strange this evening?" Robert asked.

"No," he said turning to Megan. "Did you see anything?"

Megan swallowed hard while she shook her head. "No."

Robert turned back to the officers. "Sorry, we can't be of any more help."

"Well, if you see something strange don't hesitate to call. They may be armed and dangerous."

"Armed and dangerous?" Robert said with wide eyes, fighting the urge to laugh.

"Yeah, that's what the complaint said."

Robert shut the door before the officers could ask any more questions. He walked back into the living room and gave Sara his glass of cider.

"Could I have something a little stronger?" Robert asked.

They all broke down and laughed at the absurdity of the evening. In all actuality, it started out as something innocent and then turned into the biggest fiasco ever.

Once Robert downed the brandy sour nothing that happened that evening bothered him anymore. He sat back and enjoyed the exchange between Megan and her parents. It was so unlike his relationship with his parents. He did not know if it was the brandy or just finally relaxing and being in good company, knowing that it was not going to be a difficult task asking Ben for Megan's hand in marriage. The hard part was going to be getting him alone!

It was well past midnight when the four realized the time. Sara, as a hint to call it a night, slowly gathered up the empty glasses. Megan, sensing it was time, got up with Robert following close behind. She walked up the stairs. Robert passed her and slowly walked to his room. He then waved good night to Megan and wished he could spend the night with her but knew how inappropriate that would have been.

Megan disappeared into her room and undressed but then looked at the diamond pendant around her neck. She took it off and then grabbed her robe. Megan tiptoed to Robert's door and heard MSNBC news playing on the television set. She tapped lightly on the door. It did not take long, and Robert peeked out.

"You sleeping?" Megan asked, remembering she had not kissed him goodnight.

"No. I can't stop thinking about what happened," Robert said and then grinned.

"Who would think something as innocent as going Christmas caroling would land you in trouble with the police."

Robert leaned on the door sill while he laughed uncontrollably.

"Hey, be quiet," Megan said. "My parents will hear you."

"This Christmas will always be memorable for me," Robert quipped. "Our first Christmas together almost spent in the clinker."

Megan shook her head as Robert cupped her chin and then bent down and kissed her.

* * *

Through the night, snow fell and blanketed the streets and houses with a new coat of white. It was surely going to be a joyous holiday season. Although the occupants of the house on Monroe Street stayed up most of the night, the morning sun came early, and a busy day would soon follow.

Megan woke first and quickly got dressed. By the time she left her bedroom, Robert had walked out of the bathroom with a towel wrapped around his waist. His hair was wet from the quick shower he took.

"Why don't you get dressed and meet me over there by the attic entrance?" Megan said as she pointed to the ceiling attic door.

"What's up there?"

"We're going hunting for white elephant gifts," she said.

Robert shrugged and then disappeared into his room. By the time he dressed and was back in the hall, Megan was carrying a stepping-stool and set it below the attic entrance. She climbed up and pulled the lever that released the latch that held the attic door. When it fell open, she pulled and extended the ladder down. Robert appeared amazed by how the house was structured.

"I don't get what you mean by a white elephant gift."

"It's a tradition in our family. We have to find a dumb gift for them. Something you'd normally discard."

"So why are we looking up here."

"We are going hunting."

"I still don't get it. Why give something you'd discard. It doesn't make sense."

Megan started climbing the ladder, and once she disappeared into the attic, Robert soon followed.

"You'll see."

Once inside the attic, Megan rummaged through some boxes. She came across an old picture of Uncle Jake with a woman. It appeared to be a wedding picture and judging by Jake's appearance. It was a few years back.

"This is ideal for Uncle Jake."

"What's so bad about this picture, it's a beautiful photo of the two of them?"

Megan pointed to the woman. "That's his second wife," Megan said as she laughed.

"How many times has he been married?"

"I'm not sure. I think it was three, not to mention a few who just never made it to the altar."

"Quite the ladies' man."

Megan looked at Robert and shook her head. "Hey, you are the one who wanted to meet my family. I can't help the family that was dealt me."

"I think the picture is appropriate and I get the white elephant thing now. What do you have in mind for whose name I got?"

"Aunt Judy," Megan said, and she rummaged through another box of kitchen junk.

It did not take long, and she came up with a plastic container that looked like an onion. "Good, I thought this was up here someplace."

"What is it?"

"It's for storing onions in the fridge."

"So?"

"My aunt hates onions. She's supposed to be deathly allergic to them."

"Giving her this gift, isn't that a little mean?" Robert asked.

"You haven't met my aunt yet," Megan said and then quickly added while Robert appeared puzzled, "You'll understand when you meet her. Besides, she eats ketchup like it's going out of style. If you look at the label, you'll find onions listed."

"You don't have to tell me that," was all Robert said.

"I'm sorry. I keep forgetting," Megan glanced at her watch quickly. "What time are they picking you up for ice fishing?"

"I'm not sure."

"We better get down and eat breakfast before they get here."

Megan walked over to the ladder and started the climb down. As Megan closed the attic entrance, Sara came out of her bedroom carrying a few wrapped Christmas presents. She turned to the two.

"You guys are up early," she said looking at them.

"We were just picking out our White Elephant gifts," Megan said, holding up the picture and the onion saver.

"How fitting," Sara remarked looking at the picture. "I wonder whatever happened to Cassie, his second wife?"

"I'm sure Uncle Jake would love to tell you. Didn't she take him to the cleaners," Megan said and then turned to Robert. "And I don't mean she took his clothes to the cleaners either!"

Sara hurried down the stairs. "Well, I have breakfast to make now that you two are up."

Sara disappeared down the stairs. The sweater she had on had a Christmas scene that ran all around the sweater. Robert was curious about how anyone could knit such a scene and not go crazy in the process.

Robert turned to Megan. "How many Christmas sweaters does your mother own?"

"I don't know," she said. "That was always Nana's favorite gift to give her daughters. But I don't think the other four ever wore theirs. Probably donated them to some third world country."

CHAPTER 9

Sara had been up early as there were more gifts to wrap and now there was a hearty breakfast to prepare for her guests. She knew that Josh and the boys would be there early for a day of ice fishing and it was only fair to send Robert off with something in his stomach. Once the bacon was frying, and the eggs cooked she turned things down on the stove and went to the stairs.

"Megan and Robert, breakfast is almost ready," she said and then turned back to the kitchen.

The only thing left to do was pour the orange juice and milk, not remembering how Robert liked his coffee or for that matter, if he drank it first thing in the morning, so she set the table in the hopes that everyone would help themselves.

It was not long till the two were down the stairs and found their place at the table. Sara was pleased when Robert helped himself and took the pot of coffee off the stove and poured each one a cup.

Ben walked in from the garage laden down with snow pants with a matching jacket. He held onto the boots with his other hand.

Sara turned to him. "I told you they were in the tote out there."

"I should have known you were right."

"No sense storing that stuff in a closet when you don't go snowmobiling anymore."

"I just couldn't remember where it was," Ben said. "I honestly thought you gave it to the Salvation Army last year."

"I threatened to do that, but you wouldn't hear of it."

Everyone ate a hearty breakfast. Robert was not sure when he would be eating next, so took an extra helping of eggs and bacon. It was cold out, and he regretted agreeing to this adventure but did not want to back out of spending time with Megan's cousin.

Sara got up from the table and took her plate and cup to the sink. "I'll send the rest of the coffee with you in one of Ben's thermoses."

Robert glanced up at her with a look that said thank you. He turned to Megan hoping she would come up with some excuse to keep him here, but none was offered.

"Whatever they come up to do, you stay out of trouble."

Robert was taken aback by the remark. "What could happen, we're just going ice fishing?"

"Hey, the fact you are going with those three scares me."

Robert turned to Ben. "Where can I get an out-of-state license?"

"Don't worry. You'll have to stop at a bait shop. They should also sell licenses."

No sooner than he said those words then a horn honked outside. Robert turned to the door as it honked again.

Sara glanced at the clock on the stove and then the door. "I swear your cousin and uncle have no manners."

"I'm sure Fred next door will be over to complain later," Ben said.

Robert slowly got up. He took the snowmobile suit from Ben and then quickly put it on. He zipped up the front and the side leg zippers. The horn honked again. Robert just stepped into the boots as Sara went to the kitchen closet and tossed him a knit cap. He then hurried to the side door.

"Don't forget your coffee," Sara quickly added as she grabbed it off the counter.

Robert took the thermos and replied. "I'm off to put food on the table."

Megan laughed as she gave Robert a quick peck on the cheek. "Have fun. You'll be lucky to catch a six-pack with those idiots. At least come back sober."

"It's eight o'clock in the morning," Robert replied as he glanced up at the clock.

"Yeah, and come back sober."

Robert turned and was out the door before Megan could change her mind about letting him go. She had heard horror stories of those Christmas fishing expeditions and was not prepared for Robert being invited to one on his first meeting with her family. But then maybe she was just paranoid.

* * *

Josh followed Uncle Johnny in his old beat-up pickup truck. They stopped at the bait shop and bought a few dozen minnows. Robert spent the fifty dollars for the non-resident license after a long argument with Uncle Jake about not bothering with the license. Robert knew a fine would be far worse than spending the fifty dollars and was not about to have his first trip to Wisconsin involve getting a penalty for breaking the law. He did not want to explain to Megan why he let Uncle Jake talk him into breaking the law given Uncle Jake's inclination to do so.

Once they had their bait and Robert his license, they were finally on their way to a fun-filled day of fishing on the ice. Josh slipped a CD into the slot under the radio and suddenly "Grandma Got Run Over By a Reindeer" started playing.

When Robert heard Jake open a can, he assumed it was a can of soda, but was startled when Jake handed Josh the can of beer. Jake offered Robert the next can, but he quickly refused. Robert glanced at the clock on the dash and wondered who in their right mind started drinking at eight-thirty in the morning.

Josh turned back to Robert. "We should be there soon."

"I've never ice-fished before. You'll have to show me how."

Jake laughed. "Nothing to it. We'll each set three tip-ups and sit in the truck and watch them."

"That's all?" Robert remarked. "Don't we stand over a hole?"

"We didn't come here to freeze our asses off."

Robert had a look on his face as if to say, what am I doing here?

Josh followed Uncle Johnny's pickup carefully. Robert was relieved when he saw the left blinker go on hoping that they were finally close to where they would be spending the day. Josh followed too close, and Robert feared a rear-end collision. Robert breathed a sigh of relief when they came to a small lake and Uncle Johnny's pickup quickly veered off the road onto the frozen body of water. Robert's eyes suddenly got wider. It had not occurred to him they would be driving vehicles on the ice. He just thought they would walk to where they would be fishing. They followed Johnny, who was fishtailing all over the place. Slushy ice was being thrown up into Josh's windshield, and for a moment they could not see.

"Asshole!" Josh yelled as if Johnny could hear.

Josh pulled along side of Johnny's pickup, and the two raced to a group of shanties on the ice in the distance.

Both vehicles were neck and neck, leaving a trail of wet slush behind them. Josh had one hand on the wheel. The other hand had the beer can. He quickly took a swig of the beer. Robert just shut his eyes while quickly making the sign of the cross and said a prayer hoping to come out of this day alive.

Once they reached the ice shacks, both vehicles slowed down and they quickly found a spot off in the distance and parked their vehicles.

Josh quickly got out and opened the back hatch. He took out the Jiffy ice auger and cranked it up. Within a few minutes, Josh drilled nine holes. While he put the ice auger back in the vehicle, Jake started getting the tip-ups ready. Josh grabbed the minnow bucket out of the vehicle and started putting the bait on the hooks and setting the tip-ups in the holes that were drilled.

Uncle Johnny had his setup and quickly drilled three holes for himself. He then checked the depth, and once that was established, he set up his tip-ups.

Robert sat in the back seat while Josh and Jake were in the front seat drinking their beers. Robert observed the tip-ups and hoped above all else that a flag would go up, so he had an excuse to venture out. His coffee was long gone, not for warmth but more as a pretext to not accept a beer. He had never known anyone who drank beer that early in the morning and now he understood Megan's reluctance at him going on this fishing expedition. In reality, it was just a way to get out of the house for Josh and Jake, but Robert did not need an excuse. He enjoyed being around Ben and Sara. Most of all he enjoyed being near Megan and spending the day talking to her.

The radio played funny Christmas songs non-stop since they started fishing. Josh turned to Robert in the backseat.

"It's your turn to check the tip-ups."

Robert was thankful for a chance to get some fresh air and quickly went outside. One by one he checked each tip-up. It was a beautiful day with temperatures in the mid-thirties. He was thankful for the fresh air, as he was getting stiff just sitting in the backseat, and only hoped they would not be fishing much longer. He did not care about the fifty dollars he spent for the license. Right now a day at the mall was more appealing than sitting in a truck watching the two grown men drink beer all morning.

Robert glanced at Uncle Johnny's truck as Johnny got out and drilled three more holes. Robert just assumed a fishing buddy was showing up soon.

Suddenly a flag went up on one of their tip-ups. Robert ran over and grabbed it and pulled on the line. Josh and Jake came running out of the truck and over to him.

"Set it, set it!" Josh yelled.

"Set what?" Robert looked up at him, not knowing what he was talking about.

Josh grabbed the pole and line from Robert. He quickly yanked up on the line and then handed it back to Robert. Robert struggled to pull the line up out of the water. Finally, Robert pulled a six-inch perch out of the hole.

"That's hardly a mouthful," Josh said and then laughed.

Johnny finished setting up his three extra tip-ups. Josh reluctantly put the perch in the bucket. They walked back to the Explorer, and when Robert got in, he had to fan the air to get rid of the stench of what the two had been smoking while he was outside.

Josh and Jake resume drinking their beers. Again Robert declined and felt bad for being a party pooper but did not want to face Megan with beer on his breath. In the distance, Johnny disappeared in his truck.

"Where did he go?" Josh asked as he pointed to Johnny's truck.

Robert glanced in the direction of where Josh was pointing, but there was nothing to see in Johnny's truck. He wondered if possibly he collapsed.

"Is he okay?" Robert asked.

"Oh yeah. He's okay alright!" Jake said.

Jake and Josh cracked up laughing, as suddenly there were two people in Johnny's truck. Robert was startled for a moment, and even more surprised when he realized that it was not a person, but an inflatable doll sitting next to Uncle Johnny.

"What the...?" Robert snapped and then stopped quickly.

"I was wondering about the extra tip-ups."

"Is that legal?" Robert questioned.

Josh laughed as he turned back to Robert. "What do you think?"

Uncle Johnny got out of his truck with the inflatable doll. The inflatable doll was wearing one of Uncle Johnny's team bowling shirts. They walked arm in arm to where the tip-ups were set. Once Johnny checked all six, he and his inflatable doll walked back to his pickup truck.

Robert was puzzled. He turned to Josh. "Why did he do that?"

"In case a warden is watching."

"And a game warden can't tell it's an inflatable doll?" Robert asked not wanting to appear stupid.

"You want to tell Uncle Johnny that and burst his bubble?"

Robert closed his eyes and then shook his head in disbelief. "I guess not."

Jakes reached in the cooler. "Shit. We're out of beer. Let's go over to Papa O'Mally's to get more."

Robert thought that Jake meant a bar or something, but Josh and Jake got out of the vehicle. Josh turned to Robert and motioned for him to follow. Reluctantly Robert got out and followed the two to the shantytown. They stopped at a somewhat large shanty with a satellite dish attached to the roof and a generator humming out back. Robert guessed it had to be at least ten by ten. Josh tapped on the door before entering.

"Come in at your own risk."

Josh opened the door, and the three walked in. Robert glanced at the four guys playing cards in the center of the room. There was a thirty-six-inch flat screen television on the wall tuned to a sports channel. A portable fridge sat in the corner, and a potbelly stove with kettles of food simmering sat next to it. Robert just stood in awe. Off on one end was a two-foot opening that extended the length of the cabin where twelve holes were cut and tip-ups set. Bart, a friend of Josh's, looked up from his cards.

"Didn't think Sandy would let you out of your cage."

"Hey, I'm the man of the house," Josh argued.

"Sure, if that's your story and want to stick with it. That's your choice. What do you guys need?" Bart asked.

"Some beer if you have extra?" Josh begged.

Bart motioned to the fridge. "Six-packs are in the fridge. But I expect it replaced."

"I'm good for it," Josh said.

Bart glanced over at Jake. "Didn't think we'd see you until spring."

"Not much going on, so I decided to come in for the holiday."

Bart looked at Jake and then at Robert. "Who's your friend?"

"My niece's boyfriend."

"Josh, remember you still owe me a six-pack from last season."

Josh nodded as he went to the fridge. It was stocked with shelves of beer. Josh pulled out a six-pack.

They were soon walking back to their vehicle, and no sooner than they were inside, Jake opened two cans of beer, knowing full well that Robert would not be drinking with them. Jake took out a joint and rolled it. He quickly lit up and took a long drag and then exhaled. He handed it to Josh who did the same. Robert was left in the back seat just watching the two and praying for an end to this outing.

"What if a warden comes?" Robert asked, but this fell on deaf ears.

Both Josh and Jake laughed. An hour passed, and by that time, they were both either stoned or drunk. Jake handed Robert the joint. Robert, in turn, rolled down the window and tossed it out. He fanned the smoke out of the window the best he could. Josh's phone suddenly started ringing. Josh fumbled with it, and it fell between the two men. Robert quickly reached between the two seats and recovered the phone and answered it quickly.

"Josh, my water broke. I think it's time," Sandy yelled.

Robert turned to Josh, who was passed out behind the wheel. Robert shook his shoulder, but Josh was too far gone to be revived.

"Sandy, this isn't Josh," Robert said pathetically.

"Hurry, I have to get to the hospital and you know I can't drive, not in my condition."

"But," Robert argued but knew it was useless arguing. It was a life or death situation, and he had to act fast.

The phone suddenly went dead. Robert in a panic glanced out the window at Johnny's pickup. He quickly jumped out of the vehicle and hurried over to Johnny. He opened the driver's door and pulled Johnny out.

"You take care of those idiots. When Josh comes to, tell him the baby's on the way. I'm going to see to it that Sandy gets to the hospital."

Robert jumped into the driver's seat. Once he got the pickup started he sped off the ice and then down the highway.

The inflatable doll was still sitting in the passenger seat, secured with the seatbelt. Robert laughed to himself. At least he would not get pulled over for a seatbelt violation, he thought. As an elderly couple passed him on the two-lane highway, Robert realized they were staring at him and the inflatable doll. He was just thankful that they did not know who he was. Robert reached over and released the seatbelt and then struck the inflatable doll, trying to get it under the dash, but instead, she bounced around the cab and landed up in his line of vision. The pickup swerved in and out of lanes of traffic. Robert managed to roll down the window and struggled to push the inflatable doll out of it. Finally, Robert was able to get the legs out of the vehicle and then pushed on her head and sent her flying out onto the road. The inflatable doll bounced head over heels down the highway until it landed precariously in the ditch.

Once he got the pickup under control, Robert reached into his pocket for his cell phone and quickly punched in some numbers.

"Megan. We got a call from Sandy. She's in labor. Would you go over there to make sure she gets to the hospital? She can't drive herself."

"Where's Josh?"

"Don't even ask. I'll meet you at the hospital," Robert replied and was about to end the call and then rolled his eyes. "Oh yeah. You have to give me directions. I'm coming in on," he hesitated a moment and then saw the sign, "I'm on 29 East coming into town."

Megan gave Robert the directions as quickly as she could trying to remember the best rout for him to take to the hospital. Finally, she rushed out the door and headed for Josh's apartment. She only hoped Robert listened carefully and could get to the hospital in time to meet her and Sandy. She didn't want to be alone with Sandy while she was in labor.

Robert pressed the end button and then put both hands on the steering wheel and stepped on the gas. He was thankful that there were signs along the highway guiding him to the hospital and with Megan's quick directions, he felt confident that he was going in the right direction.

CHAPTER 10

Robert quickly drove around the hospital parking lot before noticing the sign for a birthing center and figured that would be where he would find Megan and Sandy. Once he parked the pickup, he noticed Megan's rental car parked near the entrance. Megan was bending over the passenger door while helping Sandy out of the car. Robert quickly got out of the pickup and rushed over to the rental car. Sandy was out of the car with Megan on one side of her. Robert took the other arm to steady Sandy who doubled up when another contraction came on.

The three walk up to the emergency entrance, with Sandy stopping between contractions which were coming minutes apart. When the pain subsided a little they took a few more steps until the next contraction started up again, Sandy turned to Robert.

"Where's Josh? Ow...ow..."

Robert turned to Megan and whispered. "He wasn't in any shape to be here."

It didn't take long, and they were finally standing in front of the door to the emergency entrance. Sandy's contractions were coming closer together. She hung onto the railing as one started coming full force. The three had to stop and wait for the contraction to subside before going any further. Meanwhile an orderly seeing them coming rushed out with a wheelchair.

"Give me something for the pain," Sandy yelled.

Megan took Sandy's hand, "Honey, we haven't even gotten into the delivery room yet. Just hang in there, only a few more steps."

Quickly Sandy was placed in the wheelchair and rushed through the emergency entrance and passed the nurses station.

"I think they'll want the contractions a little closer along before they give you anything," Robert replied as Sandy was already down the hall with Megan trailing behind.

Sandy squeezed Megan's hand to the point she too was in pain. Megan turned to Robert and looked at him helplessly as she and Sandy disappeared through the doors leading to one of the emergency rooms.

* * *

Sandy was in the straddled position to give birth. Robert and Megan were on either side, giving Sandy directions on breathing. The doctor sat at the foot of the bed giving everyone instructions on what to do next.

"Push," the doctor ordered.

Sandy's face tightened and turned beet red as she pushed hard. Megan held onto her hand while Sandy squeezed it tightly causing Megan to wince in pain too.

"The head's out!" the doctor said, glancing up at Sandy. "Stop pushing for a moment."

Sandy relaxed a moment before the final contraction came.

* * *

Josh, Jake, and Johnny hurried into the birthing center reception area.

"My wife Sandy was brought in," Josh yelled, not even remembering to tell the receptionist her last name.

The receptionist just pointed to the waiting area where the three reluctantly went. The smell of stale beer was an indication of why they had to wait there and not be ushered to the birthing room where Sandy was delivering the baby.

* * *

Once the baby was born and all the details of her birth documented, Sandy was given her baby and had it resting on her chest. Robert stood next to Megan. He had his arm around her and hugged her tightly. It had been an experience he would never have given up for all the tea in China, as the old saying went.

"I never saw anything so beautiful," he said.

"I didn't think I had it in me."

"You were great." Robert kissed Megan on the cheek.

Sandy glanced up at the two. "I want you two to be her godparents."

"But I thought Cousin Missy and her husband were going to be the godparents," Megan added as she took hold of Sandy's hand.

"The way you two were there for me, I want you there for the baby too."

Robert had a pleased look on his face. "We would be honored," he replied and then turned to Megan. "We better get going, your parents are probably worried."

Reluctantly Megan let go of Sandy's hand. She suddenly felt a kinship with Sandy. Even though she had only known Josh's wife for a short period, she knew they would be friends forever. It would always be something that they shared, and no one could ever take that away from them.

Robert guided Megan out of the room, leaving Sandy alone with her daughter. They slowly walked down the long hall hand in hand. When they passed the waiting room, it was then that Robert remembered Josh. Quickly Josh got up and hurried over to the two.

"How's Sandy?" he asked and then looked back at the receptionist. "They won't let me in."

"She and your daughter are doing fine," Megan said.

Jake stood up and appeared agitated. He turned to the receptionist. "I want to talk to someone in charge. This is not right. He's the father. Who in the hell do you think you are anyway?"

Megan turned to Jake. "Would you just shut up? You smell like a brewery and reek of dope."

"When will they let me see her?" Josh asked.

Robert stepped forward. "Why don't you go home and get cleaned up first."

Jake moved forward and got in Robert's face. "What gives you the right?"

Robert just turned to Johnny. "Take these idiots home." Robert took hold of Megan's arm and led her to the exit.

"I take it fishing didn't go well," Megan whispered.

"You have no idea," was all Robert said as they walked outside to the hospital parking lot.

He glanced over at Josh's vehicle and stuffed in the back hatch was the inflatable doll. Robert just shook his head and laughed at the absurdity of the day.

* * *

Once Megan reached her rental car and drove out of the hospital parking lot she glanced over at Robert.

"Would you mind if we made a stop before we go home."

"You're driving," Robert replied.

Robert was glad that the morning was behind him. He did not care if he ever went ice fishing again and certainly not with Uncle Jake.

They drove in silence for almost fifteen minutes when Megan turned off the road, and Robert read the sign for Gate of Heaven Cemetery.

"You're freaking me out," Robert said wondering why they were visiting a cemetery.

"I thought if you knew where I wanted to go you'd back out."

"Who's buried here?" Robert asked.

Megan turned to him and replied. "Nana."

"Oh," was all Robert could muster up to say. Megan never really talked much about her family, so he was taking everything in because he was now seeing a side of Megan that she'd kept hidden from him.

Megan drove through the small cemetery until she found the marker she was looking for. She stopped the car and then got out. Robert opened the passenger door and followed Megan to the monument.

"I wish you could have met her," Megan said.

"You were close?"

"She watched me when I was a baby while Mom worked."

"I didn't know."

Megan wiped away a tear. "She was the glue that held the family together."

"They're still coming to your parents tomorrow."

"This will probably be the last Christmas the family will be together."

"I don't get it," Robert replied.

"You will tomorrow. There's always some dissension. Everyone always made up before the holiday for Nana's sake. But now that she is gone, I don't see anyone bothering to try to get together anymore after this."

* * *

Even though it had been a busy afternoon up at the hospital and before that the fiasco of the ice fishing trip, Robert was still enjoying himself. He had never had so many things go wrong in all the holidays he could remember. This one would truly be one for the record books.

As Megan pulled into the driveway of her parent's house, her heart sank when she saw the familiar car. She did not say anything to Robert, deciding instead to let him make his own judgment on this part of the clan.

When they walked in, Ben was sitting by the fireplace while Aunt Judy and Uncle Mike were sitting staunchly on the couch. Aunt Judy sat rigidly with lips pursed. She looked a little like Sara, but her features were hard looking and not soft like Megan's mother. Sara had on another one of her Christmas sweaters, this one with a big snowman on the front. Robert laughed to himself wondering how many of these sweaters she owned.

Robert helped Megan off with her coat and hung it in the hall closet and then took his off. They walked into the living room to join the group. Aunt Judy turned to Megan. Her jaw muscles tightened while her eyes narrowed somewhat, but her lips never let go of the pursed feature. It was always a way to broadcast when she was upset.

"Hi, Judy. Your granddaughter is beautiful."

"I wouldn't know," Judy snapped.

"Didn't you go up to see her yet?"

"I don't think it is appropriate for me to see her before her father can get in to see her."

Megan turned to her mother, who rolled her eyes while shrugging her shoulders. Megan sensed that this visit had not gone well and Robert and her showing up just then was a welcome relief to the cold shoulder she was getting from her sister. Judy was always right in every situation, even when she truly was in the wrong. But that was life in Sara's family, and it had only gotten worse since Nana passed earlier in the year.

"We left him an hour ago. I would have thought he would have gone home and changed and gone back to the hospital."

Robert leaned over to Megan and whispered, "That's if he didn't pass out first."

"He isn't still with Uncle Jake, is he?" Megan asked.

Sara, sensing the tension in the room, got up and disappeared into the kitchen. She walked back into the living room a few minutes later with a plate of Christmas cookies and fudge.

After a long silence, Judy turned to Megan. "What gave you the right to be there?" she finally snapped.

Sara dropped the plate on the table, catching everyone's attention. She stared at Judy for the longest time before responding.

"I think they tried to call you, but you were at the casino!"

Robert almost choked as he stepped forward. "It was my fault. Sandy called on Josh's phone. He..." Robert hesitated a moment before continuing. "I took it upon myself to call Megan to get Sandy to the hospital and took Johnny's car to meet her there."

Uncle Mike stood up. "And who are you?" he asked in a condescending tone.

Megan stepped between the two. "He's a friend of mine. We did the best we could."

"Well it wasn't your place," Judy added sharply.

Megan shook her head and then looked Judy straight in the eye. "You want the truth?" she asked.

Uncle Mike stepped forward and quickly snapped, "Watch your mouth, and remember I'm bigger than you."

Megan just stared at him and laughed in disbelief. Ben got up just then and positioned himself in front of Megan.

"I think we all better step back a moment before we say something we will all regret later."

Judy got up quickly, still with pursed lips. She walked over to the door, followed closely by Uncle Mike.

"We'll see you later?" Sara said sweetly.

Judy turned and just said a quick "Hum!" She was not used to someone having the last word. And indeed she was not used to Ben talking to her like he had just done. Judy had always been the drama queen in the family and everyone seemed to bow down to her every mood swings.

CHAPTER 11

Sara disappeared into the kitchen. She had to have a moment to herself and compose herself for fear she would breakdown. Sara did not want Megan to see just how affected she was by their visit. She mixed herself a stiff drink and chugged it down while the cocoa was heating up. It took just enough time to cook the mixture for her to drink the last of the vodka tonic. Once she had her composure back, she put the cups of hot liquid on a tray and tossed a marshmallow in each of the cups and started to walk out with the tray. Come hell or high water she was not going to let Judy ruin Christmas for her. Before walking out of the kitchen, she set the tray down. She grabbed the vodka bottle and poured a little into her cup.

"That went well," Sara said with a smile. The vodka tonic mellowed her mood to the point of not caring about anything just then.

"I would just love to tell her what I think," Megan said, taking the cup off the tray.

Sara looked sternly at Megan. "Now Megan, what would that serve."

"People are so worried about hurting her feelings, and in the end it allows her to walk all over everyone."

"I know. We always overlooked things because of Mom. But Mom isn't here any longer, and we don't have to let her crap on us so that we can be together for a holiday."

"Do we have to go over there this evening?" Megan asked.

"Oh yeah. She will play the martyr to the hilt. She'll want the family to side with her. I just want to be there, so she doesn't have free rein to rake me over the coals."

"Josh was drinking all morning, and when he got to the hospital, he reeked of dope. When are they going to wake up to the fact that he has a problem and it's worse when Jake's in town."

Sara just shrugged, still feeling the effects of the drink. "It's not my concern. I'm just thankful you had brains enough to get out of town and get an education."

Megan took a sip of the hot liquid. She wished that she would have gone into the kitchen with her mom and had what she was drinking because she knew she would need it to get through the rest of the day. Megan suddenly looked up as if remembering something.

"Sandy wants Robert and me to be the baby's godparents, so technically it will be our problem because I can't condone Josh's drinking and use of drugs while raising my godchild. I won't stand for it!"

Sara just raised her hands. "I don't think Judy or Mike know this. Last I heard Missy was going to be the godmother."

"How did Shelly take the news?" Megan asked knowing full well that her two cousins always competed for things.

Robert looks puzzled for a moment. "Now who are those two?"

Ben piped in at that point. "That's right. You are new to all this," he said. "They are Josh's sisters."

"Oh," Robert said, knowing now why there would be a problem.

"I'd love to be a fly on the wall for that one," Megan said laughing at the thought.

"I'm going upstairs to take a quick nap," Ben says getting up. "It's going to be a long evening."

Sara busied herself collecting the mugs and plate of cookies.

"I'll help you clean up," Megan said and then motioned to Robert to follow Ben upstairs.

Once they were alone in the kitchen, Megan turned to her mother. "Are you okay?" she asked.

Sara turned and smiled. "Couldn't be better."

"Why don't we just back out of going this evening."

"I won't give her the satisfaction this time."

Sara started the water in the sink. "You go upstairs and get ready. We'll be leaving in an hour."

Megan could sense her mother wanted to be alone and respected her need for privacy. She knew her mother did not like confrontation and always turned the other cheek when it came to the antics of Aunt Judy. Megan guessed some things would never change as she turned and walked out of the room.

* * *

Robert drove the rental car as he followed Ben and Sara in their vehicle. Megan had promised to take him looking at Christmas lights on the way home. Her parents bowed out of that outing. There was still a lot of work to do before the open house tomorrow. Megan would have Robert all to herself in showing him her favorite holiday tradition. Some houses made her father's house look like an amateur decorated the lights.

Robert turned to Megan. "I don't get it."

"What don't you get?" Megan asked, knowing full well what was to come.

"Spending the evening with your uncle and aunt's, especially after what happened this afternoon."

"It's what we always do. Have an open house at everyone's house and see their Christmas tree during the holiday season."

"You have an unusual family," Robert said with a smile on his face.

"Let's not go there. Why do you think I didn't want you here?"

Megan just shook her head knowing full well that there would be more to come.

She turned to Robert and continued. "My family is the essence for the term dysfunction. It's like we can't get along unless someone is fighting."

"But to disregard the obvious is ludicrous."

"You can't save the world. And you can't change a person in one day that's taken years to produce."

"Don't his parents see his problem?"

"I'm sure they do. They just choose to ignore it and not deal with the problem. Once you meet the sisters, you will understand."

"Why, what's wrong with them?" Robert asked.

"All I can say is Missy thinks the world revolves around her and no one other than her has feelings. And Shelly, don't talk politics or the CIA. She thinks they have this technology where they are watching and listening to her."

Robert laughed uncontrollably. "I guess it depends on how desperate they are for entertainment."

"As funny as that sounds, it's not a laughing matter. This is serious."

He turned to Megan and realized she was serious. "CIA, doesn't she know it wouldn't be them. With Homeland Security and all, it's the FBI's job to spy on the citizenry."

Megan pointed her finger at Robert. "Don't even go there. You get her on that subject, and she will try to convince you that you are wrong and we all have to worry about being watched and listened to. She even will try and convince you they can view you through your television and microwave."

"I believe they do have the technology to listen and pick up on chatter when certain combinations of words are being used."

Megan looked at him and rolled her eyes. "Robert, don't you even bring up the subject."

Robert laughed, thinking how interestingly the evening could go. But then he would have to face Megan in the aftermath. He realized as much fun as he could have with this, it just was not worth it.

Ben pulled into the driveway while Robert parked the rental car on the street. He did not want to get blocked in just in case things got a little tense with Aunt Judy or Uncle Mike.

When they walked up the drive, Ben turned to Megan. "Put on a happy face," he responded with a mocking laugh.

"Bah humbug!" was all Megan mustered up to say.

Sara turned to the two. "Besides, it is only once a year."

Megan quickly turned to Robert. "Once too often."

The small group walked up to the porch. Christmas music could be heard coming from the house. Ben was in the lead, and he quickly pressed the doorbell before anyone could change his or her mind about being there.

* * *

The house was decorated in festive colors. The tree that sat in the front window was done up in an angel theme with crocheted snowflakes scattered about, and a garland was arranged meticulously. In all actuality, the tree was perfect, with not an ornament out of place. The left side mirrored the right and could easily have made the cover of any national magazine.

Once everyone got there, each person congregated around the living room in small groups. There were plates of cookies and candy on the coffee table.

Sara nervously glanced around the room as if not knowing what to say. She spotted some snow figurines she had not seen before and turned to Judy.

"Those are lovely."

Judy turned to the figurines that Sara was referring to. "Oh those, I sent away for them from Paris, you know in France."

"Yes, I know where Paris is," Sara said in her defense.

Megan turned to her mother with a clenched jaw. Aunt Judy got up and took the photo book off the table and passed around pictures of the baby. It surprised Megan given Judy's attitude earlier, but thank goodness for one-hour processing. Judy must have worked hard to have this book ready.

"Isn't she the most beautiful baby you've ever seen?"

"So you guys made it up to the hospital after all," Megan replied trying to make idle chitchat.

Judy's lips pursed even more than before as she turned to Megan." "Why wouldn't we?" she snapped.

Sara turned to Judy while she shook her head. "Megan didn't mean anything by it." She quickly turned to the tree. "Your tree is lovely this year."

Judy let go of Megan's remark and turned to Sara. "Unlike you, I like to keep up with the times."

Megan poked her mother, not wanting the two to get into a heated argument, not at Christmastime. Sara had her own Christmas tradition, and it was the same every year. Whereas Judy worked at a department store in town. She always bought end-of-the-year clearance items and changed her Christmas theme every year.

"I like my traditional tree, and I can't see changing every year just to keep up with the latest trend, plus wasting money because I have to throw out last year's trimmings."

Ben took a cookie off the tray on the coffee table. He too did not want to see the two argue over Christmas decorations, especially not like last year.

"These are good," Ben remarked, trying to change the conversation to something neutral.

Judy perked up somewhat. "Oh, it's a new recipe I tried. There are only three ingredients."

Sara glanced at the cookies and appeared puzzled. "Only three ingredients," she repeated.

"And so easy too," Judy replied.

"You'll have to give me the recipe."

"You buy a tube of sugar cookie dough. Bake the cookie like the package shows. Then melt a bag of white chocolate chips and dip them in peppermint sticks that you crush up."

Megan almost choked and wondered if possibly Aunt Judy should have been a blonde. She mockingly said, "Three ingredients?"

Judy turned to Megan with pursed lips. "That's what I said."

Sara cleared her throat while motioning to Megan with her eyes not to pursue it and then quickly cut in, "Is Josh coming?"

"Yes, he'll be here later. He's at the hospital with Sandy. You know she'll be able to go home in a few days."

"They don't keep you in the hospital for long anymore," Sara replied.

The front door opened just then, and Missy walked in with her mousy husband, Paul. Her hair looked like a plastic cut out similar to Betty on The Flintstones. If there were a wind, not a hair would dare move out of place. Missy hung onto Paul as if afraid he would bolt. Before they could take off their coats their dog Becker, a Golden Retriever came racing into the room. He jumped on the couch climbing over the visitor's laps, sending cookies and drinks flying. And when he saw the plate of candy he made a mad dash for them, sending a few pieces off the plate. Missy turned to everyone and laughed as if thinking the whole incident was cute.

"Becker is happy to see all of you."

"That's nice, but I'd appreciate it if he stopped humping on my leg," Ben snapped trying to push the dog off his leg.

Missy just ignored Ben's request while Mike got up and walked over to the plate of cookies. He just picked up the plate and put the few cookies that got knocked off back on the plate. He then passed them around. No one accepted his offer, so he set the plate of cookies back on the coffee table while Missy took off her coat. Once that was done she turned to Megan.

"When are you going to settle down finally?" she asked.

"When I get good and ready!" Megan replied.

Missy turned to Robert. She eyed him up and down. "I see you brought a date."

"Robert isn't a date," Megan snapped, not liking how it came out of Missy's mouth. "He's a friend from Chicago."

"You should have brought him to the wedding."

"My invitation wasn't extended to a friend," Megan replied curtly.

"You must be mistaken," Judy snapped.

"I'm sure Megan didn't make a mistake, and you know how inappropriate it would have been to bring someone who wasn't invited," Sara said sweetly, trying not to offend Judy just then.

Judy's face turned a few shades of red. She avoided looking at Sara.

Sara on the other hand, never took her eyes off Judy, anxious to hear her explanation for this purposeful slight on the invitation. This was not the first time Judy did something like that, but it was the first time Sara had the nerve to stand up to her sister. In the past Sara always let it slip, but she was taking a stance now.

"I'm sure there's been a mistake," Judy responded in her defense. "Your invitation clearly should have said you and a friend."

Megan just shook her head. "Trust me, Aunt Judy, the invitation to Josh and Sandy's wedding was extended to only me and not 'and friend.' I still have the wedding invitation at home if you would like me to send it to you to prove a point!"

"Well, mistakes do happen."

Missy just turned away. "What's the big deal anyway," she said, trying to make light of the indiscretion.

Sara, although she wanted to take a stance with Judy, sensed things were getting a little out of control, and tension was high in the room. She glanced up at Ben, who just shrugged, and then finally she turned back to Judy.

"Has anyone seen any good movies lately?"

As if on cue, Becker started acting up and made a mad dash for the cookie plate again. This time cookies flew all over the living room carpet and were quickly gulped up by the hungry animal. After the dog had them all eaten, Paul got up and walked over to Becker. "I'll lock him up in the bathroom."

"No, he likes being with everyone," Missy snapped.

Paul nervously stepped back, not wanting to go against Missy. Megan had always liked him, but he never seemed to have a backbone when it came to Missy. Paul tried to change the subject away from the dog and his wife's insistence at letting him free to roam the house at will.

"Missy and I just bought the latest Reese Witherspoon Christmas movie. We have it in the car," he added. It was almost an invitation to let everyone view it as a way to change the conversation.

Sara, buying into the weak invitation, turned to him. "I wanted to see that movie last year. Why don't we watch it?" she said.

"It's my movie, and I don't want to share it until I've seen it first," Missy snapped.

"But dear?" Paul argued.

"You heard me! If they want to watch it, they can go out and rent it."

Ben's face suddenly reddened. This was about all he could take of Sara's family. He glanced at his watch and then got up slowly.

"There's no time. I think we better get going."

"But you just got here," Judy argued.

Sara, sensing Ben's frustration at how the evening was going, got up and followed her husband's lead.

"I still have a lot of work to do getting ready for the open house tomorrow."

All four walked to the entrance when the door opened suddenly, and Shelly walked in. Robert felt a little awkward as Shelly stood in his way. She just took off her coat and handed it to him as if he were a butler. He turned to Megan, who was standing nearest the closet where their clothes were hung. She opens the door and reached in for a hanger and hands it to Robert.

When Shelly's back was turned, Megan leaned into Robert, "She always thought she was to the manor born."

"Do I look like the butler?" he said and then laughed.

Shelly turned suddenly and in a superior manner took off her knit hat and handed that too to Robert. Robert looked at her as if to say, who do you think I am? He happened to look inside the knit hat and saw the tin foil. Robert tilted it so that Megan could see the foil. Her eyes widened and then she mouthed, "Don't even go there."

When the group stepped out of the house, and the door had shut behind them, Ben turned to Robert.

"What was that all about back there?"

Robert just shook his head. "For one thing, I didn't know who she was until I saw the tin foil in the knit hat."

"You are shitting me," Ben said laughing uncontrollably. "I honestly thought they were making up the stories about changing locks because she thought the CIA was searching her house. Does she believe that they can tune into her thoughts too?"

Sara just shook her head. "You know what they always say about people who feel that they are being watched. They usually have something to hide and are doing something illegal."

"Mom, you're talking about Shelly. What could she possibly have to hide?"

Sara shrugged her shoulders. "I'm just saying."

"Why don't we get the hell out of here before we get sucked back into that den of kooks," Ben said.

"I'm all for that," Megan replied.

Ben turned to Sara after glancing back at Megan and Robert.

"Next year we're starting our tradition, and it won't be visiting your idiot sister or her spoiled idiot daughter or the one who thinks everyone is watching and listening to her."

Sara just shrugged. "Right now I won't argue with you. I can't believe how rude Missy was."

"The apple doesn't fall far from the tree," Ben snapped.

"Missy has always been that way, and Judy never called her to task, so why should she change now? I remember once when she was taking Mom for a doctor's appointment Missy threw a hissy fit because she wanted to sit by the door and didn't want to sit next to Mom. Judy pulled over and made Nana sit in the back seat. After that Mom never had Judy take her anywhere."

Megan turned to Robert and just shook her head. It was the reason she didn't want him there this year. But in the end, maybe it was better that he see what he was getting himself into, if they should ever marry.

CHAPTER 12

Megan followed Ben as they traveled through town and was surprised when her father turned into the Birthing Center. She parked the rental car next to Ben's vehicle.

Robert turned to her. "I didn't realize we were going to stop to see the baby."

"I didn't either. I'm glad, though. I wanted to see her again."

"Me too," Robert replied.

Robert got out of the car quickly and opened Megan's door. He was rather enjoying Megan's family. And given the baggage they all seemed to be carrying, it only made her meeting his parents less troublesome. He now realized every family had their little quirks, but in the end, the family was family.

Quickly the group entered the Birthing Center, and before stopping to see Sandy, they walked over to the nursery to see if they could view the new addition to the family. All the babies had on tiny red elf hats.

Megan pointed. "There she is."

"Oh, she is so precious," Sara smiled warmly.

Ben put his arm around Sara. "Your time will come, and you'll have grandchildren like you've always wanted."

Robert glanced at Ben and then looked over at Megan and smiled. Tonight would be the perfect time to talk to Ben. He would just have to find an excuse for them to be alone.

Once they had their fill of looking at all the beautiful newborns, they slowly walked down the hall to where Sandy's room was. Given the majority of the family was at Judy's house, they were sure they would not run into any more of the family.

Megan tapped lightly on the door and then opened it. Sandy was sitting up in bed with Josh holding her hand. The four walked in.

"Josh, we saw her, and she has to be the prettiest baby in the nursery," Sara said, but then guessed that most family members felt that way about their newborn.

"She sure takes after her mother," Josh turned to Sandy and kissed her gently on the cheek.

"Oh Josh," Sandy smiled while shrugging him off.

Robert took a good look at Josh. His eyes were not bloodshot, and he appeared sober. Josh turned to Robert and extended his hand.

"Thank you for all you did today."

"It was nothing," Robert remarked.

Josh motioned for Robert to follow him out of the room. Megan turned to the two and appeared puzzled, but decided not to follow.

Robert did not quite understand why Josh would want to talk to him. A part of him was a little apprehensive, but the other part knew what he did that morning was right. He only hoped that Josh saw it that way. Once the door closed to Sandy's room, Josh turned to Robert.

"I want you to know I'm going to change things."

Robert was taken aback for a moment. "It's not my place to judge you."

"You were there for Sandy when I should have been. I didn't realize how much it has been taking over my life."

"It isn't going to be easy."

Josh shrugged while shaking his head. "But it will be worth it. And I promised Sandy."

Robert took Josh's hand and shook it. "I'm proud of you for owning up to your problem."

Josh nervously fidgeted with his fingers. He turned and walked away for a moment and then turned to face Robert.

"Sandy told me she asked you and Megan to be Kelly's godparents."

"I realize it was in the heat of an emotional moment."

Josh shook his head. "No. We would be honored if you two would accept. I don't care what my parents or Missy have to say about it."

"Really?" Robert responded.

"Yes, I can't think of anyone I'd rather have been a part of her life than you two." Josh hesitated for a moment and then continued, "I figure you can also keep me on the straight and narrow." Josh turned to the door to Sandy's room.

Robert patted Josh on the back as Josh opened the door to Sandy's room.

"By the way when's the christening?" Robert asked.

"End of January, if that's okay with you guys. Sandy can call Megan with the details."

"I'll make sure we free up the time."

The conversation with Josh touched Robert in a way he was not prepared for. Both his parents were only children, so he never had cousins to deal with. Josh's honesty about his problem and his attempt to get clean made Robert like him all the more. Granted, under normal circumstances he and Josh probably would never have become friends, but Robert knew that they would always have something in common and that was the love they had for the women in their lives.

* * *

Robert followed Ben carefully as he took them on the tour around the city looking at Christmas lights. He had never seen so many houses decked out for the holiday season and he wondered why his parents never took the opportunity to do things such as this. Plus it gave he and Megan plenty of time to talk. Once Ben pulled into the driveway, Robert pulled in next to him and parked the rental car.

Megan finally turned to Robert. "But is this something you want to do?" she asked, wondering if Robert said yes to being Kelly's godparent only because he got caught up in the holiday spirit.

"I wouldn't have accepted if I didn't mean it or take the job seriously."

"I can't tell you how much this means to me."

Robert leaned over and pulled Megan into his arms. He kissed her passionately.

"I love you," he whispered.

Ben tapped on the car window startling the two.

"You going to make out like that all night?"

Robert released Megan but then quickly kissed her once more. The two followed Ben and Sara into the house. It had been a busy day, and as active as they all had been, no one wanted to turn in. Megan walked into the kitchen to help her mother with the final preparation for the Christmas Day open house. Megan turned to her mother after about an hour cutting vegetables for the snack tray. She sipped her glass of wine and then picked up another carrot to make carrot curls.

"You work all Christmas Eve to get ready for the open house tomorrow. Is it worth it?" Megan asked.

"I like to keep busy. And as hectic as Christmas Day gets, I enjoy the family getting together."

Megan laughed. "At this rate, I'll still be up to go to Midnight Mass with you and Dad."

"Robert can come along too."

Megan appeared a little apprehensive. "I'm not sure he would want to."

Just then Robert walked into the room. He caught that his name was mentioned and turned to Megan.

"What wouldn't I want to do?" he asked.

Sara quickly cuts in. "Come along to Midnight Mass."

Robert shrugged. "I'd love to go. My grandparents used to take me every year."

"I didn't know that," Megan said, realizing there was a lot of things that Robert never talked about, mostly about his family and how they celebrated the holiday.

"That will change," Robert said in his defense.

Robert picked up a knife and helped Sara and Megan finish up cutting the vegetables.

CHAPTER 13

Other churchgoers attending midnight mass crowded Ben, Sara, Megan, and Robert in a pew that was meant to hold ten, but twelve were packed in now. Megan glanced around and saw Aunt Judy and Uncle Mike. Shelly was next to her father, looking around nervously to see if men in black coats were nearby. She adjusted her knit hat and Megan could only guess the tin foil inside the hat must be causing some discomfort, or she wanted to make sure it was positioned right so no one could hear her thoughts. Megan just chuckled to herself, wondering how a person could be so delusional. Missy and her husband were on the other side of her parents, and when songs were sung, Missy belted out the song as if she were on stage when in all actuality she sang the tune out of key.

When mass was over, the four quickly walked to the side door of the church. Ushers were opening the doors for everyone.

"Hey Megan," a voice came from the church.

Megan turned and saw Jeffrey. He was someone she dated years ago while she was in college and she had completely forgotten all about him.

"Jeffrey, I didn't know you moved back to town."

"Yeah, a few years ago."

Megan turned to Robert. "Robert, this is Jeffrey Simmons, an old college friend."

Robert remembered Megan talking about a Jeffrey, and from what he could recollect, they were more than just friends.

Megan turned to Jeffrey. “Robert and I work for the same company in Chicago,” she said, making it sound casual. She leaned over to Robert. “I’ll see you in the car.” It was a clear invitation for him not to stay with her and he respected her wishes just then.

But before he walked off, Robert took another look at Jeffrey, a little curious about what he meant to Megan.

Robert waited in the car with Ben and Sara, and all three just watched Megan talking to Jeffrey.

“I wonder what he wanted?” Sara asks.

“Probably regrets letting Megan go,” Ben remarked.

Robert looked a little startled. “Is he an old flame?”

“Not sure. They only had a few dates while his fiancée was away at college,” Sara said, rolling her eyes as she was not sure she should even have said that much.

“And Megan went out on dates with him?” Robert asked.

“Fact be known, Megan was under the impression they broke up. It wasn’t until he made a move on her on the second date and she turned him down that he confessed he was still engaged and was going back to Jill.”

“Oh, so he wanted to see if he could get a little on the side while his girlfriend was away at school?” Robert said under his breathe.

Ben turned around and looked at Robert in the back seat. “You catch on fast.”

They watched Megan and Jeffrey for almost ten minutes before Megan finally turned and walked toward the car. Snow started to fall in large clumps making it almost look like a snow globe outside, especially with the streetlight in the background.

Once Megan got in the car she turned to Robert. “Boy, what a jerk,” she said with a smirk on her face.

Sara turned to Megan. “What did Jeffrey want?” she asks.

“He wanted to know if we could get together while I’m home for the holiday.”

Ben cleared his throat. "Isn't he married?"

"Oh yeah. He played the wife doesn't understand me card. Like he's such a catch. My God, they have three kids, and he comes to church and hits on me thinking we can go partying after mass."

Robert looked at Megan. "He did see that you were with me, didn't he?"

"That doesn't stop Jeffrey. He thought maybe I could ditch you and meet him out later."

Robert grabbed the doorknob, but Megan quickly stopped him.

"It's not worth fighting over," Megan replied and then turned to Ben. "Let's go home now?"

Ben promptly put the car in gear and drove down the road. The roads were getting snow-covered and a little slippery. Robert took hold of Megan's hand and held it tight, reassuring her that he was not concerned about old flames. But he was not happy with the fact that the guy hit on her while he was with her and after mass, no less.

* * *

Once back at the house Robert pulled Ben aside while Sara and Megan finished up in the kitchen. Ben sat comfortably in his easy chair in front of the lit Christmas tree.

"What did you want to talk to me about," Ben asked knowing full well Robert had been trying to get him alone all day.

Robert cleared his throat. "I don't know how to say this."

"Be direct, that's usually how it's done."

"You know, then?"

"It doesn't take a rocket scientist to understand what's going on here."

Robert's shoulders slumped while he shook his head. "And you are going to make me ask you anyway?"

"That's why you came here, isn't it?"

"Ben, can I ask your daughter to marry me?"

"Now was that so hard to say?"

"No, but you didn't make it easy."

"When are you going to ask her?"

"I'll wait for the right moment, but I want to do it before we leave for Chicago."

Ben got up and walked over to Robert. He patted Robert on the back. "Good luck, son. I would have thought after meeting the rest of the family you would have run for the hills," he mocked with a grin on his face.

* * *

When Robert was finally dressed for bed, he walked out of his bedroom and tapped lightly on Megan's bedroom door. He heard movement from behind the closed door.

Robert whispered, "Megan are you still up?" Megan opened the door slowly. "What is it?"

"I wanted to ask you something."

Just then Ben walked out of the bathroom with a magazine in his hand. He looked at the two for a moment.

"Is there something wrong?" Ben asked shyly, knowing full well what Robert had on his mind. The two already had their discussion and Ben was looking forward to Robert joining the family, but he was not going to make it easy for him.

"No," Robert replied.

"What is it you wanted to ask me?" Megan said taking a quick glance at her father before turning back to Robert.

Ben just stood there waiting, which made Robert even more nervous. He was enjoying the young man's attempt at getting his daughter alone to pop the question. He remembered what it was like when Sara's father pulled the same stunt.

"It's nothing, really," Robert replied and then quickly added. "It can wait until morning."

"Are you sure?" Megan asked, a little disappointed because it seemed like it was important a few moments earlier.

Robert glanced nervously over at Ben. "Good night, Ben."

"Good night, Robert," Ben replied.

Robert turned around and disappeared into his room. Ben glanced at Megan and then shrugged his shoulders. He turned and walked back to his bedroom, leaving Megan standing alone in the hallway with a look of wonder on her face.

* * *

The next morning Robert descended the stairs with the gift-wrapped little ring box in his hand. He slowly tiptoed over to the Christmas tree that was surrounded by beautifully wrapped gifts. Robert bent down and accidentally dropped the ring box amongst all the other presents. Just then Sara and Ben descended the stairs and did not see Robert searching the boxes for the ring box he dropped.

"I wish you wouldn't have asked him to be Santa. You know what happened the last time," Sara said sternly.

"That was years ago. He didn't mean anything by it."

"Josh cried for weeks afterward."

"Who knew he would give the kid coal as a gift."

Robert quickly stood up. He looked like the cat that swallowed the canary.

"We didn't realize you were up already."

"I couldn't sleep," Robert said sheepishly.

He laughed to himself when he saw the matching Christmas sweaters the two were wearing. The bells jingled with every step they took.

Sara pointed an accusing finger at Robert. "You weren't snooping, were you?"

Robert shook his head like a little boy caught in the act but did not want to explain to either of them what he was doing.

"So, Santa is coming?"

"Yes, we're having a little disagreement on who will play him this year."

"It's Christmas Day, who are you going to get to do it this late in the game?"

"I'll let it go this year," she said with a stern look on her face. "There better not be any incident, though."

Robert followed Sara and Ben into the kitchen. Robert sat down at the table while Sara grabbed a step stool from the corner of the room and walked over to the fridge. She climbed the step stool and opened the cupboard and took out the punch bowl. Ben was at another cupboard and took out a bottle of Southern Comfort and a couple of two-liter bottles of soda.

"Wow! Looks like my kind of party."

Ben turned to Robert and laughed. "Trust me. It will make the whole day barely tolerable."

Megan walked in. She was all dressed for cross-country skiing. Megan turned to Ben. "Pop, can Robert use your ski equipment?"

"Sure. It's in the basement where we keep all of the equipent."

Robert turned to her. "Is there time?"

"I don't care. I need to get out before the crowd comes."

"I was going to sample the punch."

Megan glanced at the bottle of Southern Comfort and then glanced up at the clock and laughed.

"There will be plenty of time for that later. We're only going to do a quick run and be back in a few hours. Plenty of time to have a few cups of punch to numb you before the family descends upon us."

"You make them sound like vultures descending on their prey."

"Trust me, sometimes that's exactly how I feel."

Megan quickly went down the basement steps followed close behind by Robert. They gathered up the ski equipment and were on their way within fifteen minutes.

CHAPTER 14

Megan drove out to Nine Mile where the county had top of the line groomed cross-country trails. Robert was surprised at the number of cars in the parking lot given it was Christmas Day. But in Central Wisconsin cross-country die-hards never let a holiday cramp their outings.

Megan led while Robert struggled to keep up. Going down one of the hills Robert took a tumble. Megan turned around, and when she saw him lying headfirst in the center of the trail, she turned around to make sure he was okay. Before Megan got to Robert, she lost her balance on a small incline and fell almost on top of Robert. They both burst out laughing. Other skier's just shook their heads as they whizzed passed the couple. Robert quickly rolled over and pinned Megan before she could get up. They kissed passionately.

* * *

Megan and Robert hurried into the kitchen. Robert grabbed Megan around the waist and pulled her to him and then he saw Sara at the counter. Sara quickly gulped the remnants of her glass. Megan appeared surprised to see her mother drinking that early in the day.

"Mom?" Megan said catching Sara off guard.

Sara set the glass in the sink. She turned to face Megan but said nothing. She just had a sheepish smile on her face.

"How many have you had?"

Sara raised her hand with one finger up. But then slowly another finger popped up. Ben walked in from the living room.

Megan turned to her father. "Dad, what's wrong with Mom?"

Ben rolled his eyes. "Your Aunt Judy called. I guess she found out Josh and Sandy wanted you guys to be Kelly's godparents."

"So?" Megan said knowing full well that it was not going to sit well with her, but she just wanted to play dumb.

"You know your aunt."

"Is she still coming today?" Megan asked.

"Oh yeah! Your mother is building up enough courage to face her."

Megan laughed. "That will be interesting," she said as she turned to Robert. "I've never seen my mother this tipsy."

"Maybe she will finally let me put her sister in her place," Ben replied.

Sara reached for the punch ladle to pour herself another glass, but Megan stopped her.

"Mom, I think you should hold off for now. I'll change and help you with the rest of the meal."

Megan glanced at her father and then sniffed the air. She looked around the kitchen. It was as if a light bulb went off.

"I don't smell anything cooking." Megan turned to the oven and saw it was not on. Panic overcame her. "There should be a thirty-pound turkey cooking."

Ben shrugged. "Beats me."

"If we're eating in five hours it should have been in the oven two or three hours ago," she said and then turned to Sara. "Mom, where's the ham I bought for your New Year's Eve party?"

"In the garage fridge."

Megan quickly took off her jacket and then motioned for Robert. "Go get the ham out of the refrigerator in the garage," she said and then turned to her father. "You make a run to the store and pick up six dozen hamburger buns. Also, get a couple of large bags of chips."

Ben looked a little puzzled. “What if the grocery store is closed? It is Christmas Day.”

“Then stop at a gas station, I need at least six dozen buns, I don’t care how you get them.”

Megan quickly went to the cupboard and grabbed a bunch of cans and set them on the counter. She then turned back to both men and motioned with her hand.

“Get going,” she said and then turned to Sara. “Mom, you go upstairs and lie down. I’ll come up and check on you in a little while.”

Megan busied herself unwrapping the whole ham. It was a spiral cut, so all the slices fell nicely off the bone. Megan took a plate out of the cupboard and set a few slices on it and covered it with foil and then shoved it in the fridge. She looked at the huge turkey sitting on the bottom shelf and shook her head.

Megan grabbed three onions from the vegetable drawer, set them on the counter and then quickly turned on the oven. It wasn’t long, and she had the sauce for the ham mixed in a kettle and set it on the stove to heat.

Within a short period she had the roaster on the counter filled with ham, and slowly she poured the heated barbecue sauce on the meat. Megan covered the pan and put it in the oven. She stepped back and breathed a sigh of relief.

The kitchen door opened, startling her for a moment. Ben and Robert walk in with Kwik Trip bags.

“Great! Buns from a gas station.”

“It was these or nothing. We missed the store closing by ten minutes.”

Robert sniffed the air in the kitchen. “Whatever you are cooking, it sure smells good.”

“That Nana’s barbecue ham. It was always a tradition, so it’s appropriate to serve it in memory of her this season.”

Ben opened the fridge door and stared at the thirty-pound turkey that was taking up the whole bottom shelf. “What are we going to do with that?”

“Mom said it was a fresh bird, so I guess we can put it in the freezer and have it later in the year.”

The doorbell rang just then, startling the three. Megan glanced up at the clock and then turned to her father.

"It's too early," Megan replied with a puzzled look.

"Probably Carrie and her family," Ben said and then winced as if in pain. "Your mother invited them to stay before we knew Robert was coming with you."

"I can take the couch tonight. It's no big deal," Robert replied.

Ben looked relieved. "Thanks."

"I didn't realize the whole family was getting together," Megan said.

Other years when Carrie and her family came into town for the holiday, they stayed at Nana's. But since the house sold a few months back it was either stay at a hotel or bunk in with the family. Sara was desperate to have the family together for Christmas, so everyone was invited to stay at their house if they wanted. Thankfully now Jake did not take her up on the offer.

"It's been a challenging year for your mom since Nana passed. I guess no one wanted to give up old traditions," Ben responded.

"With Nana not being here to ensure peace, the day should prove interesting," Megan remarked.

Carrie walked into the kitchen with her husband Jackson following close behind. The kids were in the living room squealing at all the presents under the tree.

Megan turned to Carrie. "So glad you could make it."

"Wouldn't miss it for the world."

Megan turned to Robert. "Robert, this is my Aunt Carrie, Mom's baby sister, and her husband, Jackson. You'll meet the kids later."

Carrie looked around the kitchen. "Where's Sara?"

"She hit the punch early," Megan laughed.

"She must have been talking to Judy then."

"How did you know?"

"Judy has been on the phone with the whole family already."

Megan shook her head. "Might have known."

Carrie walked over to the punch bowl and poured herself a glass. "I hope you have enough for another batch."

Megan laughed, knowing full well that this was going to be an interesting day. Without Nana there to make everyone tow the line, there might just be an all-out war later on.

* * *

The house was becoming chaotic, with kids running around the living room. Some of the kids were huddled in the corner practicing how to forcibly burp while others put puzzles together or played UNO. All through the room, the adults were trying to visit. Uncle Johnny, in one of his many team-bowling shirts, was sitting glued to the television set watching the sports channel. Robert tried to pull him into a conversation but it was useless. Susan, another one of Sara's sisters, was sitting close to her husband while trying to visit with Jackson. Ben just sat in the corner of the room and waited patiently for the day to end. The doorbell ringing almost went unnoticed and finally Ben got up to answer it.

Judy, Mike, Missy, and her husband stood on the porch with Missy's four step-kids and Becker. Becker raced past Ben into the living room. He proceeded to hop on the furniture and run around the room. The kids tried to catch him, which caused a frenzy of activity.

Ben shook his head as he turned back to Missy and tried desperately to be polite.

"We didn't realize you were bringing the kids."

Missy appeared a little perturbed. "Why wouldn't we, they are family," she snapped.

"Judy told Sara that their mother had them this weekend."

"I decided it would be fun to switch with her for next weekend."

"You could have called. As it is, we have a full house."

Megan walked out from the kitchen. When she saw the room full of kids she just turned around and walked back into the kitchen.

Robert, sensing something was amiss, got up quickly from the couch and walked into the kitchen. As he walked in, he saw Megan about to pour herself a cup of punch. Robert quickly stopped her.

"What's the matter?"

"That bitch! Mom has a house full of people. She didn't need four more kids and a dog chasing around the house. Besides Mom didn't buy them anything so that Santa won't be passing out any gifts for them."

"Isn't there something we can wrap up for them?" Robert asked.

Megan thought for a moment. "Mom always has a stash of stuff in the spare bedroom. I could maybe find something to wrap."

Robert took the ladle out of Megan's hand and set it back in the punch bowl. Megan reluctantly gave it up. It would have been so nice to numb what she was feeling just then.

Robert looked at Megan sternly. "I'll tell you what. You go take care of the gifts, and I'll find something to do with the kids."

"Not Christmas caroling. We don't need the cops pounding down the door today."

"No, is there possibly a place I can take them sledding?"

"Yeah, a couple blocks away. I would love you forever if you would do that, at least get them out of the house for an hour," she pleaded.

Robert walked out of the kitchen, and as he passed Carrie, he bent down and whispered. "Would you make sure she stays away from the punch bowl?" He turned to the bottle of Southern Comfort. "Also, I'd put that bottle away too."

Carrie looked up at Robert. "You're no fun."

"At least until everyone leaves."

"Well all right, if it will make you happy," Carrie finally replied.

Robert kissed Carrie on the cheek. "Thanks."

Robert hurried out of the room and gathered up the kids to go sledding. It would be one way for them to expel some of the energy they all had.

CHAPTER 15

Robert was like the Pied Piper as the kids followed him down the block. As if Robert had not had enough of outside activities, he was thrust into the outing with eight of the older children and four of the younger ones to give a little peace to the crowded house over the holiday. It was not long when the sledding hill was in view. Luckily a few of the kids knew where they were going. When they got near the hill, the sound of kids playing filled the air. Sending the kids outside to play must have been on a lot of parent's minds judging by the number of kids that congregated around the hill.

The kids made a few runs down the hill sharing the snow tubes and sleds that were still in Ben's garage. Robert was standing near the warming shed while watching the kids tube down the long sloping hill. A couple of the kids dragged Robert over to the edge under the pretense of showing him something. One of the older boys laid a tube behind Robert. Suddenly Missy's son stood in front of Robert and shoved him backward, causing him to fall back onto the tube. Quickly the kids pushed the tube and Robert down the edge, and he went flying down the hill screaming for dear life.

Robert had never gone sledding before and found this outing enjoyable and a perfect time to let his inner child fly free. For an hour he was the only adult in his group, but after a while, Josh walked over to the warming shed while Jake drove up. Robert was at the bottom of the hill. He glanced up at the warming hut and saw Josh. Robert waved, but Josh did not see him, and it was then he noticed Jake also.

Robert slowly walked up the hill with a tube in hand. A few of the kids clamored around him wanting him to go down again, but he shrugged them off and sent them down the hill while he walked around to the back of the warming shed where Josh and Jake were. Jake stood next to his open trunk. He handed Josh a zip lock bag of something. As Robert got closer, Jake took notice. He shut the trunk lid down but not before Robert saw what was inside.

Robert turned to Josh. "You promised."

"It's only a little," Josh pleaded.

Jake, with a puffed-out chest, shoved Robert back. "Who gives you the authority to dictate?" he said but was cut off by Robert, who by that time got in Jake's face.

"What gives you the right to play God with his life?" Robert pointed a finger into Jake's chest.

"Just because you're screwing my niece, doesn't give you the..."

Before Jake could finish his sentence, Robert decked him with a right fist and knocked him flat on his ass with a quick left hook. Robert then turned around quickly to face Josh.

"You get your ass out of here before I call the cops and have you arrested," Robert snapped and then turned to the sledding hill and pointed. "There are kids here!"

By that time the kids were surrounding the small group. Josh turned and tucked tail. Robert quickly put the zip lock bag in his pocket before the kids could see what it was. He knew kids this day and age were not dumb when it came to weed or what it looked like. Robert turned to the children.

"We're going home."

A crowd gathered around Jake to make sure he was okay. Jake slowly got up with the help of a few onlookers. He brushed himself off and then waved a fist at Robert.

"You haven't heard the last of this."

Robert just waved an arm at Jake as if dismissing his threats. The kids followed Robert one by one down the street leaving Jake to his ramblings.

* * *

The kids were playing quietly in the living room. No one talked about the incident at the sledding hill. Robert walked down the stairs wearing a sweater and jeans. Judy was perched on the arm of a chair that Mike was sitting in. She had pursed lips and looked as if she was stewing over something. Missy was chomping on a cookie off the plate of cookies in front of her. The rest of the group was watching a Christmas movie on the large flat-screen television at the end of the room. Suddenly without warning, Missy belched loudly. The kids all burst out laughing.

Missy just glanced around indignantly. "Well, if you have to burp, it's not healthy to hold it in."

Carrie looked at her with raised eyebrows. "You don't have to make it sound like a foghorn, though."

Robert upon hearing the exchange smiled, as he was about to enter the living room. But then he changed his mind and quickly turned and walked into the kitchen.

Sara, Megan, and Carrie were busy getting the food ready. Megan spooned the ham into the buns. Robert walked over and picked up a piece of meat that dropped on the counter.

"I'm starving," he remarked.

Megan slapped his hand. "We'll be eating shortly."

Sara glanced out the window and appeared worried. "Jake should be here by now. I wonder what's keeping him?"

Robert glanced at Megan quickly. "Was he supposed to be coming?"

"Why do you say it that way? Did something happen at the sledding hill?"

Robert made a face that indicated he knew something. Megan pulled him into the pantry followed by Carrie. Sara was busy getting the food ready and didn't notice their disappearance, plus she had a headache and was looking forward to the day ending.

"What happened?" Megan asked.

"We had a little altercation at the sledding hill. I caught Jake selling or giving Josh some, you know..."

Carrie cut in. "Drugs?"

"Yeah."

"Then what happened?" Carrie asked.

"I stopped him, and when he said something I didn't appreciate, I decked him."

"Finally, someone with enough balls to put him in his place." Carrie laughed.

"I shouldn't have lost my temper," Robert added. Violence was no excuse for settling things no matter what the circumstance was.

"What did he say?" Megan asked.

"It's not important," Robert answered.

Carrie walked out of the room, surprising Sara, who had not realized where the three had gone and now was puzzled when she saw all three walking out of the pantry.

"The only problem is, he was going to be Santa Claus today," Megan turned to Robert and said.

Robert stepped forward. "I could do that if he doesn't show."

Carrie turned to Sara. "Please tell me Jake doesn't have the Santa suit?"

"It's in the garage. Why what happened?" Sara asked with a worried look on her face. "Has something happened to Jake?"

Carrie shrugged. "He just got a little detained and might not make it in time for gift opening."

Sara just shook her head, not caring at that point. All she wanted to do was get through the day.

"You can fill me in later."

"Trust me. I will. Now I think you have a house full of hungry people to feed."

It did not take the second call to eat because everyone seemed to have an appetite, especially the kids who were on the sledding hill. One by one they hurried into the kitchen. Once the line was formed, it did not take long for the kids to walk around the island counter where the food was placed. They quickly grabbed up the barbecue ham, chips, and salads.

After the kids cleared out of the kitchen they went back into the living room where the movie was put on pause until they were back in place, Ben quickly pressed the play button once the kids gave him the okay.

After the kids were taken care of, Sara put the punch bowl on the counter, and the platter with the barbecue ham was replenished along with the salads. Then the adults took their turns filling up their plates. Mike had three buns on his plate heaped with other food. One would think he had not eaten in a week given how full his plate was. Judy glanced at the buns on the plate.

"You know I can't eat that. I have allergies to onion."

"I have some ham on a plate for you. I just forgot to put it out."

"Well," Judy snapped. "I really shouldn't be eating it because of all the sodium."

Carrie just looked at Judy. "Seriously! You can't for once eat what everyone else is having."

Sara, forever the peacemaker, walked over to the fridge. She took out a package of ground beef.

"I'll quickly make you a hamburger. It won't take long."

Sara opened the ground beef package and took out a frying pan. She quickly fried the burger and put it on a bun and handed it to Judy, who just stared at it with pursed lips.

"Normally I only eat broiled burgers," she snapped as she looked at the burger. "You know I only eat a burger with ketchup on it."

Robert stood off in the corner waiting in line to serve himself when he turned to Megan. "Did she ever read the ketchup label? They use tons of onions every day, and you would not believe the sodium that is in ketchup."

"Don't even go there," Megan whispered as she raised her hands to stop him.

Sara handed Judy the ketchup bottle. After dousing her hamburger with ketchup, she walked over to the bowl of potato chips and grabbed a huge handful and put them on her plate. Judy pranced off with pursed lips, swinging her shoulders as if she were some monarch.

Carrie turned to Megan. "One of these days she is going to get an earful."

Sara just walked over and put her arm around Carrie and patted her on the back to soothe the ruffled feathers.

"Now, now. We only see each other so seldom. Let's not allow her to ruin it for us.

Meanwhile, in the living room, everyone had found a place to eat. Judy gobbled up her burger and all her chips and got up for another helping. Carrie walked in with a platter of barbecued ham sandwiches and a bowl of chips. She handed Judy the chip bowl.

"Here, have some more," she snapped sarcastically.

"No. I should watch my salt intake."

Carrie just looked at her and said. "Really!"

Judy glanced up at Carrie with pursed lips. There was tension between the two. All through the years, people coddled Judy. When she came for a visit, the temperature in the house always had to be just so, as Judy never liked being uncomfortable and did not care how everyone else suffered through the heat.

Now that her mother was no longer living, to keep the peace, Carrie was not going to let Judy get away with always putting herself first in her dealings with her siblings.

CHAPTER 16

Megan took Robert out to the garage where the Santa suit was hung. She helped Robert dress as the jolly man so he could be the one passing out presents once everyone was done eating. Megan stuffed a pillow into his midsection. Granted this was the first time he had played Santa, but he did have the Ho! Ho! Ho! down pat. The kids would be so excited about the big man coming to pass out the gifts hopefully they would not notice who was in the Santa suit.

Megan stepped back after putting the rouge on Roberts' cheeks. All in all, he made a nice-looking Santa.

"Now remember, no scaring the little kids," she ordered.

"Oh come on, can I at least scare the older ones?"

"I don't care what you do with the older ones, but leave the little kids alone," Megan said.

Megan snuck back into the kitchen. She helped Carrie and her mother clean up the dirty dishes from the living room and had just about everything cleaned up when Carrie walked over to the living room and laughed at the kids trying desperately to be good. Tommy, one of the older kids, peaked out behind the drapes that were pulled open. There was a knock at the front door, and he scurried back amongst the group. Ben quickly walked over to the door and opened it. The jingle of bells filled the entrance.

"Ho! Ho! Ho! Merry Christmas," Santa sang with a jolly laugh.

Ben looked surprised to see Robert, but then quickly bought into the charade, not wanting to disappoint the children.

"Santa," is all he could muster up to say and then stepped back. He turned to the kids in the living room. "Look who is here?"

Robert waddled into the entranceway carrying an enormous red canvas bag filled with gifts. He shook the bells and then turned back around before Ben could close the door. "Rudolph, you wait for me."

Megan shook her head at Robert. Not quite believing he would think the kids would buy into that remark. But actually it was the little kids who were so engrossed that all Megan could do was laugh how intrigued they were with Santa.

Robert walked across the room carrying the bag of gifts. He stepped around kids who were scattered about the room and walked over to the dining room chair that was set next to the tree. As he sat down, he gave out a jolly. "Ho! Ho! Ho! Merry Christmas."

Carrie knelt on the floor next to Santa and took on the job as Santa's elf. Santa reached into his bag and pulled out a fancy wrapped gift. Santa looked through his glasses at the name on the package.

"Tommy, is there a Tommy here?

Tommy stood up. He knew Robert was inside the Santa suit. Tommy sat on Santa's knee and bought into the act for the younger children's sake. Santa shook the box and heard a rattle.

"Sounds like coal," Robert said and then laughed. "Have you been a good boy?"

Tommy's eyes widened a moment, and then he remembered who it was inside the Santa suit. Robert gave the boy his gift.

One by one each kid got a gift from Santa while everyone took pictures. Carrie picked up the little ring box. Robert's eyes widened. Carrie handed the gift over to Santa.

Carrie got a big grin on her face when she realized what was in the box. Robert, in turn, glanced at Megan and smiled.

"Megan," he announced and then quickly added. "Ho! Ho! Ho!" while jingling his bells.

Megan appeared puzzled as she made her way across the room. She maneuvered around the kids. Megan sat on Santa's knee as she accepts the little box. She quickly unwrapped it and discarded the wrapping paper. When she saw the little box, her heart raced.

"And have you been a good girl?" Santa asked.

Megan was about to open the ring box but stopped and turned to him with a big smile. "Why, yes, Santa."

Everyone laughed as they were all in on knowing what was in the box. Megan's hand shook as she found it difficult to open it for fear it was not what she was expecting.

"Aren't you going to open it?"

Megan slowly opened the box finally as Robert whispered. "Will you marry me?"

The kids all chimed in, "Megan's marrying Santa."

Megan kissed Robert. The doorbell rang suddenly, and Ben quickly glanced over at Sara, wondering who else would be showing up this late in the festivities.

Ben turned to Santa. "Santa you have the white elephant gifts to pass out," he said as he got up and went to the door. "I'll go see who that can be at the door."

Ben disappeared for a few minutes and then walked back into the living room followed by two uniformed officers. Ben motioned to Robert. Megan got up off his lap and followed Robert to where the officers were standing.

All the kids were wide-eyed and whispering amongst themselves. "Santa's going to be arrested."

Sara stepped into the center of the room and looked sternly at the children. "Now kids, why don't we all go into the kitchen for a few minutes. There are plates of cookies."

Tommy looked at his great-aunt. "I want to stay and see what they do to Santa."

Sara grabbed him by the sweater and pulled him up and shoved him toward the kitchen where the other kids went willingly.

Everyone left for the kitchen except Megan, Robert, and Ben. The officers realized the sensitivity of the situation given Robert was in a Santa suit and there were kids present.

Once everyone was safely out of earshot, Ben turned to the officer. "What's this all about?" he asked.

The older officer consulted his notes. "There was an altercation at the sledding hill this afternoon."

Ben turned to Robert, who appeared a little embarrassed as he sighed, not realizing it would come to this.

"I can explain."

"You'll have to do it at the station. Charges have been filed."

"Charges," Megan almost choked.

"Assault charges by a Jake Dombrowski."

Ben stepped between Megan and the officer while Sara walked out of the kitchen. Megan turned to Sara.

"Mom, Uncle Jake is having Robert arrested on Christmas."

Sara turned to the officers. "Jake is my brother."

The younger officer turned to the older officer, who looked sternly at the group and then turned to Sara.

"Madam, there's nothing we can do. He'll still have to come with us."

Megan put her arms around Robert. "I'm so sorry."

Robert just shook his head. "It's not your fault. Maybe Josh will set the record straight."

The younger officer took Robert by the arm. He started pulling him to the door. Robert hesitated a moment.

"Can I get out of this Santa suit first?"

The officer looked at his partner. "It won't look good bringing Santa in. Shouldn't we let him change first?"

Ben walked up to the group as Robert started undressing. "Don't worry. We'll get this all straightened out." Ben said.

The officer took the Santa jacket from Robert. He folded it with respect while Robert took off the pants.

Sara comforted Megan. "It is probably all a misunderstanding," she quickly added.

The officer took the pants from Robert and folded them nicely. He placed them on the jacket and then handed the folded Santa Claus suit to Sara.

Robert grabbed his jacket from the hall closet and followed the officers out the door. He was thankful that they did not handcuff him, but the fact he was put in the back of the squad like a caged animal was humiliating.

CHAPTER 17

Once the officers left with Robert, the family moved back into the living room, but it was hard to continue with the festivities. Judy sat with pursed lips while Carrie was pacing the floor. The kids went outside to build snowmen in the newly fallen snow.

"He had it coming. Josh told me how he just decked Jake for no apparent reason."

"Knock it off, Judy. You know exactly what happened and it had to do with Jake's side business."

"Oh?" Judy said with a look of surprise.

"Yes, and it is time you deal with it. He's dragging your son into it now."

"I don't have to sit and take this. Mike, we're leaving," she snapped and then turned to Missy. "We won't stay where we aren't wanted."

Carrie walked away with her hands raised but then turned around quickly. "Deal with it as you've dealt with everything else in your life. Go to the casino!"

Sara walked into the living room as Mike, Missy, and her sister got up to leave. The kids were still making snowmen outside, and Becker was locked in the upstairs bathroom while everyone ate.

Judy turned to Sara. "It's all Megan's fault."

Sara wiped the tears away and then stared at Judy for the longest time before speaking. "How do you figure that?"

Carrie stepped between the two. "Judy, don't start something you can't finish."

"Jake is family!"

"Yeah, and he has a problem. We all overlooked it for Mom's sake. But Mom isn't here anymore. We all have to start facing facts," Carrie snapped.

Judy just plugged her ears with her fingers. "I won't listen to this."

Mike walked over to the closet and got Judy's coat while Missy went upstairs to get Becker.

Judy made a face at Sara. "You were always Mom's favorite."

"Seriously? Why throw that into this?" Carrie snapped, not believing what she just heard.

"Because it's true!"

"And it has nothing to do with Jake and his problem!" Carrie mocked.

Sara pointed to the door. "Judy, just go. I don't have it in me to deal with you tonight."

"Hum," is all Judy said.

Judy just snapped the coat out of Mike's hand and turned quickly, leaving without putting the coat on. Missy walked down the stairs as Becker raced around the room. She immediately went into the kitchen and grabbed a large cookie off the plate on the table. She then turned to Sara and belched loudly.

* * *

Robert walked into the county jail escorted by the two officers. Jake was standing with the duty officer talking as if they were old buddies. Robert sensed that although he was on the right, things were not looking so good for him at that point.

Jake turned to Robert with a puffed-out chest as if he were someone of importance.

"You should show some respect for your elders," Jake snapped and then turned to the two officers with a smirk on his face.

"Respect is earned," Robert replied.

The younger officer took Robert by the arm. "Enough of this. It was bad enough two grown men fighting when kids were present."

"He had it coming," Robert added quickly.

Jake pointed to Robert. "He's lying."

Robert snapped his arm away from the officer and attempted to step toward Jake. "Tell them why I decked you?"

"I said something about my niece."

"Oh yeah, that was part of it. It also had more to do with what you were selling out of your trunk."

Jake went ballistic as his face flushed. He turned to the duty officer, who was finding the conversation interesting. "You going to listen to a young punk who beats up on an old man? He could have hurt me."

Robert laughed as he turned to the young officer. "Ask him what he was selling?

"We aren't getting in the middle of a family dispute."

"There's no family dispute here," Robert snapped and then turned to the older officer. "Reach in my pocket."

The older officer held up his hands. "Then is it okay for me to reach in my pocket?"

Jake screamed. "He's got a gun!"

Both offices grabbed Robert quickly and had him pinned up against the wall and frisked him. The younger officer reached in Robert's pocket and pulled out the zip lock bag of weed.

The officer whistled. "What do we have here?"

Robert turned to Jake. "Ask him! I caught him selling it to his nephew at the sledding hill."

"That's not mine. He's lying! He's a big city punk who brings this crap into our small community and causes nothing but trouble."

Just then Ben and Megan walked in followed by Josh. Robert turned to Josh. He only hoped that Josh had enough balls, to tell the truth, because if he didn't, he knew he would be in a heap of trouble.

"Tell them who gave you the marijuana?" Robert asked.

Jake smirked. "Oh yeah, get him to lie for you."

Robert turned to Jake. "Just shut up."

The younger officer stepped between Robert and Jake while Megan walked up to Robert and wrapped her arms around him.

Robert turned to Josh. "Be a man and tell these officers what happened at the sledding hill."

Josh glanced at Jake a moment and then at Robert. Robert had a concern on his face for a brief moment.

* * *

Ben, Robert, and Megan walked into the living room. Sara rushed up to Ben and hugged him.

"It's all over with. The charges were dropped," Ben said and then laughed. "You should have seen Jake's face when it finally occurred to him that he was being arrested because he sent the cops after Robert and he brought all this on himself."

"Well, I'm just glad it's over with. Judy called, she's upset."

Ben looked at her while shaking his head. "She doesn't have a right to be. You're the one who should be angry."

Carrie stepped in. "That's what I've been telling her. Jake's been transporting that crap into town for as long as I can remember. If Judy had put her foot down years ago, he wouldn't have gotten Josh into the business."

"Well, maybe now she can start taking her head out of the sand and deal with the situation."

"I'm just glad Robert was cleared and won't have a record."

Sara turned to Ben. "What happens to Jake now?"

"With what he had in his car he may be looking at doing time now."

"I'm just glad Mom wasn't here to see this," Sara added, shaking her head.

Megan pointed to Robert. "Robert almost got arrested and hauled into jail because of Jake and his lies."

"It's over with," Ben said taking hold of Sara and hugging her for support.

Megan walked away while she shook her head. She regretted allowing Robert to come home with her.

"The whole family is to blame for looking the other way about Jake's problem," Ben added finally.

"Enough of that blame game. Let's just be thankful that it's finally out in the open," Sara said with relief.

Megan walked up to her mother and wrapped her arms around her.

* * *

The house was silent as everyone went to bed early. Large snowflakes fell making a beautiful end to a troubled day. Megan finally had Robert all to herself as they sat on the floor in front of the fireplace. Robert had his arms around her.

"It sure was an interesting Christmas."

"I'm just so sorry about what happened," Megan whispered.

"It wasn't your fault."

"I guess I wanted to prepare you more before meeting my dysfunctional family."

"I don't think you could have prepared me for what happened," Robert said and then laughed.

"I'm just glad it's all over with, and we can go home tomorrow."

Carrie walked in with three glasses and a bottle of wine. She handed a glass to Robert and Megan.

"It's snowing hard out there."

"I hope the planes are flying. I don't want to chance seeing Judy tomorrow."

Carrie uncorked the bottle and was about to pour the wine into the glasses.

"Trust me. I don't think Judy will show up as long as I'm here. And it has nothing to do with what happened."

"I really would like to toast our engagement," Robert added as it to change the subject.

Robert raised his glass and waited for Carrie to pour the wine when they heard sleigh bells outside. They put the glasses down and quickly got to their feet and rushed over to the window and looked out while Ben and Sara came rushing down the stairs.

"I've got a friend who does sleigh rides. I wanted the two of you to have a pleasant memory of your first Christmas together," Ben said with a smile.

Carrie walked over to the bottle of wine and picked up two glasses. She handed them to Robert. “It’s cold out there.

Robert quickly went over to the hall closet and grabbed Megan’s jacket along with his.

The horse-drawn sleigh skimmed along deserted streets. Robert and Megan sat snuggly under a warm wool blanket and enjoyed the view of Christmas lights. Robert had his arm around Megan. Christmas music played on an iPod that the sleigh driver had in his pocket, and all was well with the world for that moment in time.

The End

Now that you have finished my book, won't you please consider writing a review? Reviews are the best way readers discover great new books. I would truly appreciate it."

ABOUT THE AUTHOR

I live and grew up in Central Wisconsin. I'm starting a new phase in my life. After being a displaced worker I've decided to take my hobby of writing to a new level and be self-employed. I'm tired of depending on others. In 2003 I was one of the writers featured in an American Movie Classics special titled Malkovich's Mail. Of the five writers and stories reviewed mine was the only one that had positive reviews, it was titled Blue Moon Rising. I did just the reverse, where I adapted my screenplay into manuscript form because it was a story that had strong characters and elements.

There is a wealth of stories to tell and I am looking forward to sharing them with all my readers. After spending a few years writing screenplays I've discovered my first love is writing novels. I will be downloading my seventh one soon.

I do appreciate comments on how you enjoyed my stories.

Here is a listing off all the books I have available.

Under the name J.J. Franck

1501 Parcher Place - Drama

The house at 1501 Parcher Place stood beautifully preserved for years. But it held mysteries of its past residents that only Trish Morgan, a recent divorcee, can uncover. Trish had done a term paper years earlier and

befriended the last descendent of the Parcher's. This friendship leads to an inheritance that turns Trish's life in a tailspin of despair when she discovers a past resident also haunts the house. In order to get peace back in her life she must untangle the relationships that led to a love triangle years earlier.
Trish struggles to rid herself of her deadbeat husband while solving the disappearance of Robert Parcher years earlier.

Raven - Political Thriller

Raven is a story about a homicide detective, Don Morgan, who while investigating the death of a brutally murdered woman, Raven VanBuren, becomes obsessed with her portrait. Raven was the personal assistant to a missing Senator which seems to complicate the situation. When Raven turns up alive Don has to face the fact that she is now his prime suspect in a murder and knows more than she is letting on about the disappearance of the Senator. This story is set in Washington DC and leads Don into the world of high stakes political financing and uncovers campaign monies being diverted into Super Pac funds that only Raven has the information to uncover its meaning. Don can only hope while solving the mystery he can keep Raven alive in the process.

Into the Darkness – Psychological Thriller

Lydia refused to die. After being brutally beaten and buried in a backwoods swamp. A lightning bolt striking a tree nearby jolts her back from the dead. The problem is she has no memory of who or why anyone wanted her dead. In the hospital another attempt is made on her life but no one believes her. Rather than go home, she voluntarily admits herself into St. Lucia Psychiatric Hospital in order to be safe and allow herself to uncover

what she doesn't want to remember.
Through her therapy sessions, Lydia soon uncovers a family in turmoil, and greed. Where murder is the only way out of past deeds done.
Shadows in the Night – Mystery (coming soon)
This story is about a terminally ill woman who is befriended by an undercover detective. When the detective is brutally killed and haunts the woman, she tries to uncover who it was who killed him so that his spirit can pass over. This is a touching story about two spirits who find love in the afterlife.

Under the name: Lillian Francken

A Family Christmas Story – Family Drama

A Family Christmas Story is a novella about one families dysfunctional Christmas celebration.
Megan Montgomery works in Chicago and is faced with her boyfriend, Robert Murphy wanting to meet her family over the Christmas holiday.
Unknown to her Robert is planning to ask her to marry him on New Years Eve, but first wants to ask her father for her hand in marriage.
Robert surprises Megan on her flight home. She is then unprepared for him meeting her dysfunctional family.

All About Love – Romantic Comedy

All About Love is a modern day version of Taming of the Shrew. If you liked Shakespeare's take on this romantic comedy you will enjoy my version as I try to follow the plot line closely.
My version has Katherine being the daughter of an ad executive, Edward Kincaid. While Edward is having lunch with his younger daughter Belinda, he offers Katherine's

hand in marriage as a flip remark to Peter Roditis, who Edward assumes is just a waiter at a Greek restaurant he frequents.
Peter is actually the son of the owner of the restaurant. Once Katherine joins her father and sister for lunch. Peter sees her and is immediately struck by her beauty. Before leaving the restaurant, Katherine accidentally drops her wallet while dining. Peter tries returning the wallet and is mistakenly hired as Katherine's administrative assistant.
Peter uses this to get close to Katherine and proceeds to tame the shrew with kindness. And in the end gain her love.

Blue Moon Rising – Thriller

Blue Moon Rising is a thriller about a small town sheriff, Dan Harter who is a widower raising a teenage daughter in a town that nothing seems to happen out of the ordinary. His major task in life so far has been keeping the single women in town at bay, while fielding calls about a marauding herd of razorbacks that had been terrorizing a local farmer.
It all changes when he gets a call to investigate the brutal death of a young teen. With the help of the new coroner, Nancy Davie, they uncover the possibility that a serial killer had been hiding in their little community for twenty years.
While investigating the case, Dan comes to realize that his dead wife might have been on the trail of the serial killer.
As the body count grows, he is drawn closer to Nancy Davie and comes to realize that his libido didn't die with his wife.

Omega Factor – Suspense Thriller

Omega Factor is a suspense/thriller about an ex-CIA agent, Sara Blaine, who is trying to hide from her past. Unknown to her the brother of her ex-lover, Mitch Winthrup was sent to protect her because an international terrorist is on a mission to kill the remaining members of the elite CIA group she was a member of.

After a failed mission years earlier, Sara was badly injured and with the help of her uncle, she faked her death and now hides with her son at her uncle's resort in a small rural community in northern Wisconsin.

This story moves back and forth between northern Wisconsin and Langley headquarters where Prescott Sinclair, a statistician at the CIA uncovers a link between a terrorist searching out and killing members the elite CIA team known as Omega, he notifies his supervisor who is more interested in advancing his own career than protecting former agents. Prescott takes it upon himself to save the last remaining member of the Omega group. There is a race against time to find the terrorist while protecting Sara from harm.

Rustic Roads – Suspense Thriller

Rustic Roads is a suspenseful story about Susan Jessup who travels to a small rural community for a week long vacation in the hopes to put her life back together after a failed relationship. Her mother is also concerned about Susan's stepsister who was on a bike tour of Rustic Roads around the state and headed for an aunts summer home on Half Moon Lake. Susan's stepsister was last heard from heading for Half Moon Lake on the final leg of her bike tour and hadn't been heard from for over a week.

Susan is swept up into the lives of the local town people and finds herself attracted to a local man who could possibly be involved in her sister's disappearance along with his own sister's death.

Tetris – Murder Mystery

Tetris is a paranormal story about a computer illiterate woman, Anna Webster, who is trust into the world of industrial espionage when she receives a copy of a game disk, Tetris and accidentally pulls up a spreadsheet tied to the game.
Anna is troubled when one of her co-workers is killed and her roommate beaten to near death. This forces Anna to seek shelter at a cottage owned by her employer, Edward Armbruster.
It isn't until the next generation computer she has access to at the cottage she is renting, helps her uncover the spreadsheets hidden in the Tetris directories on the disk. Anna along with the computer, uncovers the lengths someone has taken to siphon the company profits and bring it to near total collapse.
While communicating with this next generation computer Anna finds herself strangely attracted to the artificial intelligence that seems to have a mind of its own.

The Curiosity Shop – Romantic Comedy

Witches can be found in the most mundane place. The Curiosity Shop is a story about Cassandra Sinclair who is a dutiful niece helping an elderly aunt through a medical crisis by managing her aunt's oddities emporium, The Curiosity Shop. For years the rumors that her aunt was a witch haunted Cassandra, but they were rumors she never allowed herself to believe. That was until Mitch

Westfield, a local beat cop, enters the picture along with thugs demanding protection money.
THE CURIOSITY SHOP is a comedy of errors that's a family-oriented mystical story reminiscent of Bell, Book and Candle. Digging into the belief, people have powers beyond our comprehension, where good overcomes evil.

The Twelfth of Never – Espionage Thriller

The Twelfth of Never is about Gideon LaMont's struggle to control the demons hiding beneath the surface of his subconscious. The only thing he had to ease the pain was a picture of a woman he knew not how he came to having it or if she was real person, but it was the only thing he had to hang onto when the demons surfaced and the memories of a war long forgotten came back with a vengeance.
That all changed the day John Hamilton contacted the agency and wanted to turn over evidence of an attempt on the presidents' life. The floodgates of suppressed memories come hurtling back along with the knowledge that the woman in the picture he carried was real.

THE TWELFTH OF NEVER is a fast-paced, thriller with more twists and turns than a roller coaster ride as it rockets you towards a surprising climax. It is the story of a man suppressing atrocities of war until his survival depends on his coming to terms with what happened to him years earlier. It's also a story about love and forgiveness.

Till Death Do Us Part – Murder Mystery

Marriage can be a real killer. Till Death Do Us Part is a twisted tale about love, marriage and infidelity.
Two lives are changed forever because of a chance

meeting in a park on a hot summer night. It started out innocent enough, but when Megan Montgomery succumbed to a moment of passion with Thomas Fitzgerald, it wouldn't be long when her world starts tumbling in around her.
It was only through a twist of faith that the one thing Megan and Thomas wanted most in life would become a reality. But the price was dear to both, and soon Megan's life was in jeopardy because of it.

We Come In Peace – Coming of Age Comedy

We Come in Peace is a story about two aliens Zolar and Jupel who crash land in the desert near Area 51 in Nevada. They are searching for their comrade who disappeared years earlier when he was on an exploratory mission on earth. Lucky for them they are rescued by Bobby Drews, a pot-smoking teenager, who takes them home to his dysfunctional family. Bobby introduces them as Jane and John.
Because of the Star Trek convention in Las Vegas, Jane and John fit in well with the strangers that have come into town for the convention.
Complicating the situation, graduation is just months away and it is doubtful if Bobby will graduate even with a perfect SAT score.
Bobby is kept busy hiding the aliens from the commander of the base at Area 51. To fit in, Jane takes a job at a local café while John delivers newspapers.
Bobby in desperation enlists the aid of John to alter his school grades but things go haywire when the potion John creates and gives to the faculty has adverse side affects.

Wednesday's Child - Drama

Wednesday's Child is the child who is abandoned by life. This is a coming of age story about Jimmy Brewster, a homeless boy, who had been living on the streets because his father abandoned him.

When the story begins Jimmy has to make a decision about joining a local street gang. After living on the streets for months and seeing no end to his misery, he is about to give up on all the principles his mother taught him. That is until Don Rhodes, a down on his luck horse rancher steps in and forces him to make the choice to fight to live.

Together the two must find a common ground and in the end conquer the demon that haunts them both. Don is a recovering alcoholic who caused the death of his wife and son years earlier. Jimmy must finally come to terms with his mother's death. This story is about their struggle to become a family against all odds.

Made in the USA
Middletown, DE
01 November 2022

13887793R00086